Michelle Dutch lives in the great Pacific Northwest and has been writing and publishing for 50 years. Michelle has written fifteen books of poetry, three plays and two children's books. She is a woman of faith, a missionary, a grandmother, a daughter, a sister, a Tia (aunt in Spanish), and a cousin. She is also a world traveller. *Broken Dolls* is the second book in the Mary McKenzie series.

To Grandmothers Helen and Ellen, known as Big Grandma Helen and Little Grandma Ellen, I am grateful for all the things you taught me, especially about unconditional love.

Michelle Dutch

BROKEN DOLLS

AUSTIN MACAULEY PUBLISHERS™

LONDON • CAMBRIDGE • NEW YORK • SHARJAH

A CIP catalogue record for this title is available from the British Library.

ISBN 9781528921503 (Paperback)
ISBN 9781035899890 (Hardback)
ISBN 9781528925754 (ePub e-book)

www.austinmacauley.com

First Published 2023
Austin Macauley Publishers Ltd®
1 Canada Square
Canary Wharf
London
E14 5AA

The Missing and Murdered Indigenous Women USA works daily to advocate for Indigenous peoples in Canada and the United States, helping to bring the missing home and offering support to grieving families. They have a monthly program that includes education and self-defence lessons at every meeting. Through the voices of experience, they possess a passion and a heart for the assaulted, trafficked, or murdered women. Support through education of younger and younger women can reduce the numbers of women lost forever. They are a nonprofit organisation that is run on grants and does accept donations. Please support them in this important work.

Contact: *http://mmiwusa.org/* or follow them on Facebook.

"We extend our left palm upwards, to symbolise reaching
back to receive teachings
From the Ancestors and those who have travelled before us.
We are given the
Challenge and opportunity to live these teachings. We also
have a responsibility to pass
Those teachings to others who may also be the younger
generation, which is shown when
We put our right palm downwards. In the circle, we join
hands in respect, reverence, and cooperation."

*Vincent Slogan, Musqueam First Nation Elder (re-storied by
Jo-Ann Archibald)*

**Applying Indigenous Research Methods: Storying with
Peoples and Communities
Routledge Taylor and Francis Group New York and
London**

Prologue

He resettled the body against the wall and adjusted the mask one more time. He stepped back looking at the tableau he had created. The old woman's body let out a series of stentorian farts marked by an odorous smell that filled the space. Nothing bothered him. He used careful judgement so that anyone who entered the pueblo would immediately recognise the Kachina doll she represented, Ogre Woman or *Soyok Wuhti*. Her large mask with her red tongue pointing down her face, huge eyes and rows of fierce teeth was one of his favourite Kachinas. His attention to detail was a driving force for perfection in his tableaus and a sense of pride in his art.

Her white hide boots and cane completed her outfit. He took the basket of corn and dropped it, scattering the corn around the room. He placed a handful of corn into the grinding bowl and set the grinding stone near it. He stepped back once more with a critical eye for the details and felt replete. His skill and gifts in creating Kachinas was evident in his third tableau.

The old woman was one he had known since childhood. She had joined in beating him and he had never forgotten her laughter or his shame. When he had taken her, she had not pleaded or begged for mercy. She had simply spat in his face when he raped and beat her to death. He had brought her here to the small pueblo buildings knowing she would be found the next morning. The Hopi would know what she was. Just another broken doll.

He had been raised in the Hopi way when his mother was murdered, and then abandoned and given to his Navajo father. A man who scorned the Hopi and the Hopi way of life in all its spiritual aspects. His father had scrubbed him over and over trying to clean his Hopi blood from him.

The tribal police would be called. And nothing would be done, because the new department did not have the money or the resources to deal with him. He could go on creating his special Kachina dolls. He would exorcise his Hopi blood. He would create a Navajo Kachinas for tourists as his father had. But… his soul, was Hopi. Like his mother.

He took one last look and turned to go out the hide door. He stood in the dark watching the first rays of the sun coming over the red hills. Yee Naaldlooshii felt his body start to transform from his wolf-self to his human form. He straightened up and looked toward the red mountains. He breathed the clear, clean air, beginning to chant and sing. He danced in front of the pueblo, an eagle feather in one hand and a rattle in the other, until the dust began to lift, his voice rising up the canyon walls in an eerie sound like the wind. When he finished, his whole being was suffused with peace and calm. He walked to his beat up old red truck and climbed in. On the third try, the engine turned over and he put it into gear, rolling across the dirt roads and disappearing into the desert landscape between the Hopi Reservation and the Navajo Reservation. Just another ghost.

Chapter One

Mary McKenzie, a famous romance novelist, rolled to her side to pick up her thermos of hot coffee. She poured more into her mug, then stretched luxuriously on her chaise on the balcony of her private suite. She was on board the ocean liner, headed for the glacier at the end of Glacier Bay. On the lower observation decks, the tourists lined the rails, cameras ready for a close view of the glacier. For once, their conversations were muted as they stood in awe. The ship slowed and began a 180-degree turn so that everyone could view the glacier.

The glacier was a startling white, with deep, clear blues in the crevasses, showing eons of clarity and pureness. Ageless and ever pressing forward, it was awe-inspiring to be so close to the massive wall of ice. Segments would break off as if in slow motion and plummet into the water, raising a wave of opaque water that would create a wave that shuddered past the hull of the ship. The large ones would draw an unexpected sound of surprise from the people on the observation deck.

Mary watched in awe and reverence, amazed by the glacier. The door to her balcony opened and Special Agent Matthew Michael Gryffin came onto the balcony and sat in the lounge chair beside her. He watched the glacier for a few moments and then realised Mary's eyes were on him. He was dressed in warm grey wool slacks and a V-neck sweater that fit his rugged upper body like a glove, a gift from Mary. Her eyebrow arched in question.

"I just got a call. It's from the field office in Flagstaff. There's been another murder on the reservation. The jurisdiction is the Hopi tribal police. But because this is the third… they don't have the money or the manpower to deal with it and have asked for help. This is very unusual, and they want someone with my… experience to handle the liaison and work up a profile. It's a real tricky situation." He stopped talking, seeing hurt in her eyes.

"How are you getting there?" she spoke softly.

"FBI is sending a chopper for me. Then a puddle jumper to Anchorage. Then a flight to Flagstaff." He looked into her eyes. "I'm sorry."

"How's the shoulder? Are you ready to go back? Your headaches?" she asked, concern showing in her voice.

Gryffin took Mary's hand. "I'm sorry. You know I want to stay. I'd prefer to be here. But I can't let them find out about us. We have to keep 'us' separate. It's my work…" his blue eyes pleading with her.

She leaned forward a finger to his lips. She swung her legs over the side of the chaise and took a hold of his hands and had him stand up. "How long? Before the chopper gets here?"

"About an hour, it'll meet us after the glacier…"

Mary was immediately in his arms, kissing him. His great need filled him, and he surrendered and began walking her back toward the stateroom. He turned and pressed her against the door jam, opening the door with the other hand. She began shedding her clothes, never breaking their connection for very long. Gryffin tripped on his pants and Mary giggled, pulling him down to the bed. His mouth rarely left hers and an urgency in both of them made their movements quick. They were soon naked and turning upon the bed. He stilled her and pulled back to look into her eyes. Gryffin began to slowly kiss her cheeks, her eyelids, her ears, her neck. Mary arched her body to avail herself of every touch. His hands began to stroke her arms, her ribs, her hips and her thighs, memorising every part of her. He moved beside her and pulled her close to his chest. Stroking her nipples with his fingers, he then lowered his mouth to capture first one and then another, tugging with his lips, his teeth and his tongue until she began to moan and shiver.

Gryffin moved down her body kissing and licking her skin, tasting her, setting her every movement and sigh to his memory. He kissed his way over her hip, the scar of her surgery and to her mound, the centre of her being. Slowly she opened to him, and he teasingly ran his fingertips along her thighs, kissing and nipping until she was begging him. He began to loosely insert his fingers between her legs, and she arched against him as he kissed her very centre using his lips and tongue to induce her greater desire. He loved the way she roused to him, her open expression of passion and her response to his lovemaking.

Mary cried out his name and he rested his cheek against her thigh as her release shuddered through her body. Gryffin felt the satisfaction of knowing he had pleased her. He gave her but a few moments and then began kissing his way back up her body, stroking her side and then settling her on her back and hovering over her before entering her body.

"Gryffin!" she gasped while wriggling against him to try and pull him closer. He stopped, made her look fully into his eyes before plunging into her. Her climax began the instant he entered her, and she was calling out his name as he rode her until she clutched at him, and his own completion came with a thundering shudder that shook them both to their cores. Gryffin had collapsed on her and then shakily lifted himself to his elbows.

Her beautiful green eyes looked at him with affection and repletion. As they matched breath for breath, she smiled at him. He rolled to her side and pulled her into his arms. She rested her head on his chest while she regained her breath and tried to allow her heart to come back to a normal pace. He stared at the ceiling, his heart aching at the thought of having to leave her. This, between them was so new and had only begun a few weeks ago, when he received a text message from a cell phone number he didn't recognise.

Gryffin had still been in Seattle recovering from his injuries and feeling more than a little sorry for himself, missing Mary with every fibre of his being and at the same time being angry with himself for failing so miserably in the middle of the crisis that had almost taken her life again.

Gryffin had replayed that scene in his head a thousand times: the day he had almost lost her for good. He remembered leaving the elevator. Mary hesitated in the lobby, while Hege and he stepped into the small courtyard in front of the hotel and alley and into the chaos. In hazy memory, shots were fired from a gun muffled by a silencer, the man with the tattoo shooting, Gryffin struggling to get his piece out of the holster, reaching for Mary as she came through the oscillating doors with Rick behind her, more shots and Hege going down, trying to pull Mary behind him and then the blow to the back of his head and bitter darkness.

Waking two days later in pain from his dislocated shoulder, and adding the two-week headache from a severe concussion, he endured meetings with neurologists about his migraines and the brain injury, and more medicine for the headaches and no word from Mary.

Gryffin had been feeling desolate when the text came through on his work phone and so he called immediately. The anonymous voice on the other end told him to get a burner phone and to remove the information from his phone. He went downstairs and down the block and had a new burner within an hour and called the number again, and Mary answered.

"Hey Gryff," she spoke softly.

He couldn't breathe for a moment and then with a catch in his throat exhaled quickly.

She heard his response and answered in a hurry. "I know. I had to lay low for a bit. I had someone check on you every day. I… just needed a bit of time…"

"It's good… to hear your voice. I thought I wouldn't… I thought maybe you blamed me. After I promised…" his voice trailed off.

"Stop. I'm an idiot for not getting in touch with you sooner. But after the funeral I was pretty much on lockdown and then on a plane and in New York for a week and a half. In meetings with lawyers and financial people trying to figure out the mess Adama had made and… Oh Gryff." Her voice broke.

"Mary. Where are you?"

His voice was ragged and sounded desperate even to him.

She hiccoughed and then said softly, "I'll have a boat waiting for you at Edmonds, where we dropped you off before. Can you come today?" She paused. "Can you come now?"

"I'll be there in sixty," was his response and he left his apartment with nothing more than his go-bag and a duffle.

The meeting on the dock in front of the ocean house on Centre Island had been classic. Gryffin jumping from the speedboat onto the dock and Mary running into his arms without hesitation and without doubt. They had embraced and he lifted her into his arms, never breaking the kiss until he had let go of her when he couldn't breathe anymore.

They had walked hand and hand, laughing, climbing the stairs into the house and into her bedroom. They had been alone in the house on Centre Island for a month while Hege was recuperating from her plastic surgery with her parents in Denmark. Rick was in Hawaii with his lover Maxim recovering from his injuries and trying to repair his love affair. A relatively new and silent crew of security was still in the house, but they remained purposefully invisible while Gryffin and Mary spent time together, never leaving the house.

They made love slowly, ate when they were hungry and went out on the skiff and talked. They slept late and lay in each other's arms. The one thing they did *not* talk about was the day Maurice Dupree had kidnapped her and dragged her through the Pike Place Market intending to kill her. Veteran police officer Justis Smith had saved her. Justis had given his life for hers. The FBI had closed her case. She had moved on. But Gryffin, she was not willing to let go of.

Knowing they both had to return to work soon, Mary booked them on a short Alaskan Cruise and set them up in an exclusive suite where they could have privacy. Until today.

Mary knew that Gryffin's job was important and high profile and had to be separate from their relationship because it was a conflict of interest to be involved with a victim of a crime he was investigating. No one at the FBI could know about his relationship with her.

And for the sake of privacy, she had to maintain her own public image of being single. Anyone near her immediately underwent intense scrutiny from the public. Paparazzi constantly followed her and photographed her wherever she went. Even on-board the ship they had eaten in their state room and did not appear in public together to maintain their privacy.

There was always a feeling of immediacy and desperation, as if they both could not get enough of each other. Even when one of them would leave a room, they quickly came back together. Both of them experienced life threating events, with Mary almost dying in a vicious attack. The attack that had brought them together in the first place.

There was a discreet knock on the door. And for a moment, Mary's face was crestfallen, wounding Gryffin's heart. He rolled over and went to the door. "I'll be there in a few minutes."

He began to get dressed in his suit and tie. Mary got up and got dressed too. He threw his clothes into a bag and turned to kiss her goodbye. Mary stood looking at him and shook her head.

"I'm walking you to the chopper."

She had put a scarf over her hair, worn sunglasses and a long wraparound coat. They opened the door and two of Mary's security guards were there along with two crew members. They were quickly escorted down the stairs to the main deck, through the crowds and back up the stairs to the helipad. The chopper was inbound, the noise deafening.

In the beauty of the Alaskan wilderness, the wind chilled even in the bright light of day, Mary held tight to Gryffin's arm until the chopper landed, the wind whipping their faces. Gryffin looked down into her face and she nodded at him. The words had never been spoken, but for them both, their connection was as visceral as sharing the same heart.

The chopper door opened, and Gryffin left her side and walked to the chopper tossing his bag up inside and then climbing in. The chopper took off as soon as the door closed.

As the chopper rose, the wind swirled harshly, pulling the red scarf from Mary's hair sending it floating and dancing on the air currents to disappear over the side of the ship.

Chapter Two

There was an agent sitting across from Gryffin in the helicopter as Gryffin put the headset on. Gryffin tried to switch gears mentally, still smelling Mary on his mouth and hands, finally reaching across and taking the folder offered. He opened the page and stared at a series of crime scene photos. He looked through the paperwork seeing that the murders had taken place in the Hopi Nation. There were very few notes with each location. He looked up at the agent and asked, "Where's the rest?"

"That's it. The tribal police are not equipped to run crime scenes of this nature. They don't have the money or the personnel. They were trying to manage it on the Res."

"Am I going to the current scene?"

The agent looked pained and shook his head.

"Already cleaned up."

Gryffin growled under his breath.

"You'll need to make arrangements for me to see each of the murder sites. Where the bodies were left. I'm also going to need a crash course in native culture and customs. Can I speak to the tribal police as soon as I land?"

"There's the rub. You have to meet with the Tribal Council first, and Hopi Law Enforcement Services will be there. They have some rules that we'll have to follow. The Hopi took over law enforcement from the Federal Government in 2019. Since then, they've been running their own office. Limited budget and personnel notwithstanding. Very proud people. They are going to have to be with you every step of the way. They will have one liaison officer with you at all times."

Gryffin frowned and looked out the window at the snow-covered mountains, the cruise ships lined up in the water… "ETA to Flagstaff?" he asked.

"We'll be in Ketchikan in about two and a half hours. Puddle jumper from Ketchikan to Anchorage for about two hours. Flight from Anchorage to Flagstaff is seven and half hours."

Gryffin closed his eyes and put his head against the headrest. Then he dug out his laptop and began searching the Hopi and Navajo tribes, looking at maps, history, local newspapers and land management records dating back years. By the time he landed in Flagstaff, he felt he had a good grasp on local customs and information. He also had a migraine that was blinding in its scope. He was taken to the local FBI building which was mostly deserted and given an office. He immediately sat and wrote some notes in his journal, took some of his medication and then went downstairs to sign out a car.

Gryffin checked into his hotel and dropped his bags. He had picked up the files the FBI had given him and set them on the table to go through with dinner. He ordered room service and called the valet to come for his dirty clothes.

Gryffin had a meeting set up with the Tribal Elders and the Tribal Police, early next morning. He checked his burner phone for messages and found one from a blocked number. It was a photo of the glacier taken over a pair of long bare legs with exquisitely painted toenails.

Gryffin smiled and then jumped in the shower. Standing under the hot water until his muscles relaxed and carried away the scent of their lovemaking and all traces of Mary; his mind was racing over the case notes and the research he had done. He really wanted to get out to the kill sites and look them over, but that would have to wait until the morning. Even in the few pictures, he could see the perp had been exquisitely detailed in his dressing of the dolls. Very detailed.

He came out of the shower and heard noises in his room. He realised the waiter had let himself into the room to set up. Gryffin took his gun out of the holster and was holding it behind his back as he cracked the bathroom door open.

The waiter turned around with the check in his hand.

"Will there be anything else, sir?"

Gryffin did a brief sweep of the room with his eyes and responded, "Yeah, just give me a moment."

Gryffin closed the bathroom door, set his weapon on the counter, and pulled on a pair of sweats. He opened the door again and checked the room with his eyes and then came and took the proffered pen from the waiter. The waiter smiled and left the room. Gryffin walked to the door and put the deadbolt, chain, and door guard on. *'That was careless,'* he thought. He was remembering the serial killer who had followed him to his apartment months before. He couldn't let his guard down for a moment. Not for him. Not for Mary.

Being with Mary and her team he had relaxed his own vigilance. That wasn't a good idea. He checked the food and brought his gun into the room from the bathroom counter. He lifted the lid on the meal and sighed. Being with Mary had spoiled him. He checked his waistline in the mirror. Sometime in the gym was certainly a good idea. He went to the window and looked out at the lights of Flagstaff. He missed Mary. He went back to the burner phone. No messages. He sat down and ate his meal, feeling lonely.

Chapter Three

It had been too easy to gain access to Agent Gryffin's room. He wasn't sure what he had been looking for or expecting, but there was no trace of Mary in his things. The bag held dirty clothes and little else. There were his medications. Clearly, he had migraines left over from the attack. There were three levels of medication for Gryffin's migraines including an injectable. He smiled, glad Gryffin was suffering.

He didn't get a chance to look at Gryffin's phone, as Gryffin had taken it into the bathroom. He was amused that Gryffin had greeted him with a gun held behind his back. As if that could ever stop him. He had been onto Gryffin since he left Alaska. He really wasn't interested in interacting with him. He was just checking in. Making sure things were still the same.

He already was in the room next to Gryffin's and had stolen a pass key to get into the room whenever Gryffin was out. The thing to remember about Gryffin is that he was meticulous. Must have been his military training. Gryffin was sending his clothes out to be cleaned. So, he had taken one pair of boxers. Always good to have some DNA and a scent for future use if necessary. He was precise in planning for the future. Shadowing Gryffin was a new pastime and hobby for him. 'They were similar,' he thought.

No tokens of Mary. He was glad but secretly disappointed. He hadn't been able to get near her in months. How was Gryffin communicating with her? Must be a second cell phone. He planted the usual listening devices. He knew that Gryffin was more astute than other people, so he used only the best devices and hid them very well. He had other places to be, so he was quick in and out. He'd come back in a couple of days to check on them.

He had other fish to fry. Other people to control and manipulate. The local trucker for one. All part of the larger plan.

Chapter Four

Gryffin was to meet at 5:00 AM with the FBI agent who had been talking to the Hopi. Gryffin had been told not to dress in a suit, but rather in jeans and boots, and to wear a warm jacket. The FBI agent was waiting in the parking lot in front of the hotel in a four-wheel drive Land Rover that looked like it had seen better days. It was bright yellow with roll bars and a light rack over the front of the roll bars. It came with a winch and trailer hitches front and back and it was covered in dust.

The agent had a cowboy hat on his head and a big fleece-lined jacket over jeans and cowboy boots. He was tall and dark-skinned with jet-black hair much longer than FBI standards. He was wearing a T-shirt that said '*I'm a Fed*' and he was on the thin side but had a wide set of shoulders filling out his jacket. He had a gun on his hip and there was a shotgun in the rack inside the rover. His badge hung around his neck, and he had a huge grin on his face when Gryffin walked out of the hotel. He held out his hand to Gryffin and they shook.

"Special Agent Gryffin. I'm SSA Tom Evehema. Traitor to the Hopi or spy for the Hopi. No one knows for sure. We've got a way to go. I have coffee in a thermos. I'll fill you in on our way out to Keams Canyon, that's where the Tribal Council offices are. You'll meet the council and the new chief of Tribal Police there. There's no doubt going to be a ceremony. They don't allow white men into certain areas or villages. Wherever you go, you have to have a tribal escort. That may be the Chief of Tribal Police or one of the other officers for tribal police. If they're tied up, you have to take a tribal council member with you."

Gryffin nodded.

"How many are on the council now?"

"Twenty-two council members from the villages Upper Moenkopi, Bacavi, Kykotsmovi, Sipaulovi, First Mesa Consolidated Villages and Mishongnovi. There are four villages that don't have a representative on the council. The representatives of the council are elected by the community or sent by appointment from the village leader. They serve a two-year term. Hopi Government is a unicameral government where all the powers are vested in the Tribal Council. There is an executive branch and a judicial branch, but their powers are limited. All that to tell you, *nothing* happens on the Res that is not talked over and voted on and argued over. You can only go where you are *'invited'* to go. You can ask, but you have to wait until they agree you can go there."

"I understand why Federal Officers are not welcome, but why aren't you, the liaison?"

Tom looked uncomfortable.

"They don't trust me, regardless of where I was born or grew up or who my parents are. I'm a Fed. Fed equals betrayal and untrustworthiness. I try to walk the narrow path and I always hope for the best."

"Does that mean you have some influence? With the council?"

"Absolutely none. I'm going to be as welcome there as you are."

"You don't live on the res?"

"No. I have an apartment in Flagstaff."

Tom paused before going on. "This is kind of my first assignment. They assigned me because I'm Hopi." Gryffin made a face.

"Were you on the scene at any of the murders when they happened?"

"No. I was brought in after the second murder. But they wouldn't let us on site until they 'cleared' them and even then, the access was limited. The FBI was not called out until after the scene was 'processed' by Hopi Tribal police regardless of what the Feds wanted or asked for. The scenes were certainly… not processed appropriately."

"What changed?"

"People got nervous." He stared off for a while. "The different villages got together to meet and decided that something had to be done and it would be better for the Feds to handle it. There's a lot of strange things going on and no one wants to deal with it."

"Do you think they know who's behind this?"

Tom was quiet for a moment. He looked troubled.

"Honestly? Yes. But will they give him up? I don't know. They are private people. We typically don't talk about issues with outsiders, or our family histories. Hopi try to preserve what happens in our tribe to tribe only. Our myths and legends are private and secretive. Only for the Hopi. We just don't share 'tribal problems' with white people, let alone the Feds."

They continued the conversation as they climbed into the Rover and headed through town to the freeway. Taking in the open air and chill from the wind, Gryffin allowed his mind to wander a little, looking over the houses and buildings of a modern city until they were soon out into the desert traveling east on I-40. They travelled north on AZ-87 and then east again on AZ-264. At each junction and line of the map, Gryffin closed his eyes and saw the lines marking the reservation borders. Complicated by years of travel, fighting, secret ritual and fierce pride, the Hopi were the only tribe to never sign a federal agreement. That spoke volumes to him about who they were and how they should be approached. And they had lost more and more land until they had become an island nation surrounded by the Navajo. Complicated was an understatement.

A little after 8:00 AM they came into Keams Canyon and stopped at the 'Keams Canyon Shopping Centre', a one-story Quonset-hut building topped by a sign that was almost bigger than the building itself. Tom turned the engine off and got out of the Rover, stretching his arms over his head, the bones in his spine popping audibly in the breeze coming off the desert. Gryffin, still stiff in his shoulder, was wearing very dark sunglasses to hide the glare from his sensitive eyes. He also stepped out to gingerly stretch the muscles in his shoulder and lower back.

"We'll grab some water and snacks and then head over to the council chambers. The bathroom's at the back of the store."

"Thanks."

They walked into the store and there was no greeting from the man behind the counter or from the three men standing at the end of the counter, whose eyes followed them through.

"Bill," said Tom, in greeting to the man behind the counter. He did not acknowledge him.

Gryffin went to the back and used the facilities. When he came out, he grabbed a couple of bottles of water and some jerky. As Gryffin was paying the man behind the counter, the cashier gave him the total and then looked right through him as if he didn't exist. One of the men said under his breath, "Fed." Gryffin heard him.

Gryffin looked straight at the man and smiled. Then he pulled back his coat, showing his badge and gun. He took his change and walked out to the Rover, standing next to it while drinking some water. He turned to look up at the two mesas forming the canyon, and the few houses and double-wide trailers, surrounded by nothing but sagebrush, creosote and stunted cottonwood trees. Beyond that, an occasional new building. Opposite the highway, a road leading up a mesa with a few homes, mostly desert with scrub trees and nothing but the highway.

Tom came out a few minutes later and the three men from the store followed him out onto the porch. Nothing was said, but the threat was implied. In the back of his mind, Gryffin registered the fact that someone was in the parking lot trying to start their truck. It took them three tries before the engine turned on.

Keeping an eye on the men, Gryffin saw Tom turn back to the men and wave as he climbed into the Rover. The three men stared stonily at him as he backed the Rover up and left the parking lot, getting back on AZ-264. Gryffin quickly popped a couple of his migraine meds and washed them down with water, his sunglasses firmly in place.

Chapter Five

The Hopi Tribal Council had kept them waiting in the outer lobby for over an hour. There was a very weak stream of cool air from an overworked air conditioner near the chairs they waited in. When they finally allowed them into the council room, they spoke only to Gryffin directly and never looked at Tom. Their faces were unemotional and very serious. They addressed their concerns and boundaries. The federal government was not welcomed. All areas were off-limits until Gryffin had been cleared to go into them. Gryffin had observed a Tribal Police Chief and his deputy standing quietly to the side, waiting for the council to finish talking.

He observed the deputy. She was a beautiful Hopi woman, unusually tall and graceful even with her boxy uniform and bulky utility belt. She stood with casual ease, her eyes never leaving Gryffin's face. He tried to look away from her dark eyes and realised he felt more under scrutiny from her than the council. The council seemed to look through him. His eyes flicked back to her. She looked reserved, yet a little curious. '*Years of practice*,' he thought. Tom spoke and asked about them visiting the crime scenes. The council shifted uncomfortably and then the Chairman of the Council, Tim Nuvangyaoma, answered.

"You may go with Deputy Talayumptewa. She will show you the places. Make sure that you are respectful of our dead. Do not enter any Hopi dwelling after you have seen these sights without being cleansed. Do not take anything from any village or home, not a rock, not a part of a bush. Do not touch any animals or people with your hands. You may take pictures of the sites, but do not take pictures of any persons. Even if they will permit it." His voice was stern and clear.

"Do not under any circumstances speak to any media or newspapers. We want copies of any reports you write to your supervisors. You may give those to our Chief of Tribal Police. When you leave the Hopi reservation, you must stop the Rover and step out. Shake the Hopi dust from your boots. You must do this each day you come onto the Hopi Reservation." Tom was looking irritated, but Gryffin simply nodded in acquiescence.

The Chairman stopped and looked at each of the other representatives, making eye contact with all of them. "A Medicine Man has come to smudge you and pray for you so that the spirits from where you are going will know you for who you are and will try to protect you."

Another man entered from the back of the room wearing a mask and native costume, his body covered so that his age was undetermined. Gryffin noted he was tall but stooped over and moved as if he were old. He had a clay bowl which held smoking sage and cedar, he was shaking a rattle decorated with feathers. He was moving forward in a shuffling, rhythmic dance and speaking quietly in Hopi so that the words were not discernible to Gryffin. He stood completely still until the Medicine Man had circled him three times. Then the man stopped singing and marked Gryffin's head with a smudge of white ash. He pulled a medicine bag on a leather thong, an amulet of brown leather with a small fetish hawk sown on the outside with a bead of turquoise and a bead of rose quartz, and put it around Gryffin's neck. Gryffin had to bend down for the necklace to be placed even though he was sure the man could have reached it.

"Do not take this off until you are finished with this case and do not come back to Hopi land when the case is done. We hope the ghosts of the dead do not follow you."

Gryffin nodded solemnly and then suppressing an unusual need to bow, turned and left the council room with Tom and walked outside to the Rover in the parking lot. Gryffin looked at Tom and was about to speak when Tom silenced him with a look. Gryffin turned to see the young woman deputy coming out of the Council building talking to the sheriff. She held her hat in her hand as she spoke to the chief, although her eyes were on them. Her back was ramrod straight, a long single braid down the centre of it. Gryffin felt her gaze in the pit of his stomach. She was beautiful and sensual in an almost spiritual way. The Chief finished speaking to her and turned and left, getting into an older police cruiser with 'Hopi Law Enforcement' written on the side. She watched him drive off and then put her hat on her head and walked towards Tom and Gryffin.

She looked at Gryffin and her eyes moved from his feet to his face with undisguised interest as she walked. Gryffin was slightly startled realising the vibe she was sending him was sexual in nature. Tom seemed a little discomforted too. Without speaking, she walked past the men and climbed into the Rover and into the back seat. Tom and Gryffin climbed in. As they closed the doors, Tom turned the ignition on and then headed back out onto AZ-264. "Officer Talayumptewa, this is Agent Gryffin. How are you doing, Tally?"

Tom watched her face in the rear view. Without turning to look at him she said, "I'm good, Tom. Agent Gryffin? How long have you been on the job?"

Gryffin shifted, his shoulder aching.

"A little over ten years now."

"Always a profiler?"

"Yes, that's my specialty."

"Specialty."

There was quiet for a moment and then she turned to look at him. "You were in the papers a couple of months back. Killer in Seattle." It was a statement. Gryffin wasn't in the mood to talk about it.

"Nice ice breaker, Tally. How's your mom?"

She paused before answering. "She's well. You know where the latest scene is?"

"I'd prefer to start with the first site," Gryffin stated, looking forward and not wanting to make eye contact with her.

Tally shifted in her seat. Tom nodded without comment, put the Rover in gear, and headed out. After about ten miles of silence, they came to a dirt road and Tom turned onto it, raising a huge dust cloud. He slowed down and they stayed on the rough dirt road going over the crest of the hill and then down a steep embankment into a valley. Gryffin was watching the surrounding area and seeing and taking in the colour and beauty of the desert. It was peaceful here. The Hopi were peaceful people. Why was this happening here and now?

Chapter Six

There were a set of pueblo ruins at the bottom of the road against a cliff that rose some two hundred feet above them. Tom stopped about fifty feet from the abandoned pueblo. No one moved. Gryffin adjusted his sunglasses, waiting for the dust to settle around the Rover before getting out. He stepped out, taking in the terrain, the small birds flitting into the pueblo, the clouds scudding across a blue sky. He took a deep breath of clean, fresh air, full of sage and creosote and something else he didn't recognise.

Slowly he started to walk the perimeter, keeping his back to pueblo. He moved around cactus and scrub oak, over rocks and branches, sage, and creosote. Tally watched him closely and then started to soundlessly follow a few feet behind him. There were multiple tire tracks crisscrossing the dust in front. He stopped by one set of tracks and took his phone out of his pocket. He took a bill from his wallet and laid it next to the tracks. Gryffin took two or three close-ups of them and then stepped over them and went to the back.

There was a small gulley behind the pueblo, which he carefully began to walk down. He spotted a bright dot of colour in the grass and called to Tom, asking for an evidence bag. He pulled a pair of gloves out of his pocket and put them on and then squatted next to the piece he found. It was a small doll, a *Kachina* no bigger than 4 inches. Brightly painted once, but worn as if held by a small child. Some of the paint had come off after being held and loved for a long time.

Gryffin took several pictures of the doll where it lay and then picked it up and put it in a bag. "I'm going to have to ask you for that." Gryffin was startled a bit when he realised that Deputy Talayumtewa had come soundlessly behind him while he was working. Recovering, he stood up, sealing the top of the bag. Not giving it up right away, he adjusted his stance. He was several inches taller than her. He was attempting to intimidate her.

"The *Kachina* is evidence for your multiple murders."

Her voice in answering was clear but soft-spoken. "In Hopi, the word is *Katsina*. There is no 'ch' sound in the Hopi language. We started making *Katsina* dolls to teach our children. Like the one in your hand. The Tewa, Acoma Pueblo, Laguna Pueblo, Zuni, and Navajo also make them, but they call them *Kachinas*. It's easier on the tourists."

"You have a local lab?"

"No. But you know that. Everything goes to the Federal Labs at Quantico. Because we don't have much of a budget, we only send the highest priority evidence to them to be processed. Because of whom we are, it seems our evidence takes longer to process." She stared at him and then she held her hand out.

"Do you want to solve this case?" Gryffin's voice was flat, her face was reflected in his sunglasses.

She hesitated. "I have to do what the Council and the Chief of police tell me to do." Gryffin wished he could see her eyes behind her aviator glasses.

"You look like an intelligent, ambitious woman." Gryffin let that hang there for a few moments.

"You can always log it later. I'll overnight anything we find and send copies of the reports to your email. You can do whatever you need to make it into a report once we have the information." He looked at her for a moment. "What do you want me to call them and refer to them in the reports as, *Katsina* or *Kachina*?"

A huff of laughter escaped her.

"I think for clarity for the Fed's, stick to *Kachina*. What do you think you are going to find on the *Kachina*?"

"DNA." Her hand fell and Gryffin tucked the *Kachina* into a small leather bag he was carrying that also held a crime scene processing kit. He looked again at the place he found the *Kachina* and saw a single footprint deep on the other side of the gulley. "He's revisiting the sites."

"Could be kids," she said.

"Their footprints are in the front. These are from behind. These are his."

She frowned and then nodded. She watched him closely as Gryffin continued to walk counterclockwise around the perimeter. Gryffin was aware of her close proximity but tried to focus on what he was doing. He found a wrapper from food and asked Tom for another bag. He photographed it in situ and then put it in an evidence bag.

"You don't know how long that has been out here," she commented.

"You are correct," he said not looking up at her. "But if he brought it with him on the first pass or when he came back, we might have DNA. DNA ties a perp to the scene. The level of degradation of the DNA also gives us timelines and habits.

Where did he buy the food? Where did the bag come from? Pattern and habit defines our killer." Gryffin realised he was teaching... and that she was curious, wanting to learn.

"Or catch the teenager who came out here to ghost bust the scene with his buddies." Tom smiled broadly at them both. Tally did a large eye roll and waited patiently as Gryffin went back to his grid search again. They followed him back around to the front of the pueblo as he stood looking into the doorless dwelling. Gryffin stood looking at the front and then turned his back on the door and looked out from it. He looked at the landscape and vista of the valley. There were green plants running along the bottom of the canyon. Both Tally and Tom turned in the direction he was looking and tried to think as he did.

'*His perp lived here, felt connected to the land, and loved it? Conflicted?*' he thought.

Across the canyon, there were some flatter areas higher up where someone could sit and view the front of the pueblo. Gryffin made a mental note to go up there next. Finally, he stepped to the doorway of the pueblo and looked in. A piece of errant crime scene tape flapped from the fallen-in window. Only half of the pueblo was still sheltered by the roof. The floor was hard packed dirt and very scuffed with the marks of many feet. The ground in the centre of the room was stained dark brown. Gryffin took the crime scene photos from his bag and took one out to compare. There were only four photos of the crime scene. None were taken from the doorway.

The first photo had been taken from the corner of the room towards the body. One had been taken on the other side of the room. Again, not straight-on looking at the body. One had been taken from behind the body looking down onto it. The last photo had been taken by the back corner of the room looking out the absent front door. He had the strange feeling that the photos were not so much crime scene photos but something else, something more *spiritual* about them. He looked into the corner of the room where the roof had caved in. Several pieces of wood lay crossing each other, but not as if they had fallen. They looked arranged. There wasn't as much dirt over the top of them as there should be to match the other debris that lay in the room.

"Deputy?" Gryffin called out. He turned and saw Tally hovering at the doorway. She was looking at him intently but nervously. He looked at her, his curiosity aroused. "Did they move anything in here after they removed the body?" She shook her head. He pointed to the debris.

Her eyes roamed over the pile of rubble and then in a moment, her eyebrows shot up.

"There's a camera bag in the Rover. Will you bring it?" he asked.

She turned away and was gone for only a couple of minutes. Tom stood outside the door staring in. Again, Gryffin was wondering why he hadn't entered the room. Tally came back to the doorway and stood holding the bag out to Gryffin, but she didn't enter the pueblo either.

Gryffin crossed to the doorway and took the camera bag from her. His head was pounding as he turned his back to them both. Instead of putting the bag on the ground and possibly further contaminating the scene, he slung it over his other shoulder and opened the bag pulling out the camera. He flicked it on and did a test shot and looked into the screen and determined he'd need an extra flash to reduce the shadows. He pulled the extra flash from the side pocket, removed it from its case, put the case carefully back into the same pocket. He attached the flash unit, turned it on and did another test shot. He looked at the screen and was satisfied with the result.

Stepping back to the door of the pueblo he began methodically shooting the room the same way he would walk a grid. Tally's eyes were watching everything he did, and he sensed she *was* trying to learn. Maybe wondering if he was disturbing the scene.

He focused on the job, ignoring his feelings, his fatigue, the pain and his questions about the behaviour of the two native officers and the situation regarding the murders. Gryffin was feeling angry and frustrated. Taking a deep breath, he centred his mind and body. When he got to the pile of debris, he carefully shot it from all angles before stopping and speaking to the two still outside the doorway.

"We need to lift this debris one piece at a time. I need help to shoot a photo each time you move a piece of debris." He turned to look at them and frowned when neither moved into the room automatically.

They both stood in the doorway and looked at each other until Tom walked forward, muttering under his breath, "I guess it's me, since I'm already a ghost."

Ignoring the comment, Gryffin handed Tom another pair of gloves. Slowly, piece by piece, Tom lifted the rough wood that had been part of the roof. Gryffin had given him a piece of chalk from his kit to number the wood before he stood them neatly against the interior wall. It was quiet as each piece was moved, punctuated only by the sound of the camera shooting and a flash circling the room with light. They were down to the last two pieces of wood when Gryffin lifted the camera away from his face.

"There's something underneath the wood."

Startled, Tom carefully started to lift a heavier branch and saw it. A piece of blanket stuck up through the earth, something that was buried beneath the rubble, buried in the dirt of the pueblo. Someone had scraped at the hard dirt making a shallow grave, and then buried something there, covering it with loose dirt and then putting the wood from the ceiling on top of it. Tom's hands were shaking a little. Gryffin turned and walked to the doorway.

He spoke to Tally. "There's another body here," he stated bluntly. Tally's face broke into a look of surprise before stepping back and removing the hand-held walkie from her utility belt. She turned it on and took a deep breath. "Officer Talayumptewa to Chief Saufkie. Chief, go to channel three." She looked down at her walkie and switched to channel three.

"Saufkie here. What's up Tally?"

"Chief… there's another body at the site of the first murder. Can you send the truck out to retrieve the body?"

Before he could answer, Gryffin stepped up to her and took the walkie from her hands. Tally took a step back as Gryffin spoke into the walkie. "Chief Saufkie, I think it's time the FBI took over here. I don't want to talk over this channel, can you come out?"

There was a pause. "Yes. I am on my way."

Gryffin handed her back the walkie. "Set up a perimeter. And Tom. Move the Rover back up the road so that no one can get past you unless I OK it."

While Gryffin pulled out his work phone and called the FBI ERTU unit, giving them directions and GPS coordinates from his phone, Tom, and Tally both pulled medicine bags from their pockets and said a short prayer before the door of the pueblo. Then Gryffin called the FBI office in Flagstaff to let them know what was going on, requesting more agents to cover the scene.

Finally, he turned and walked back into the pueblo and started taking more pictures. Tally shivered although it was sunny and warm. She was overwhelmed by the degree of thoroughness Agent Gryffin had for the crime scene and overwhelmed by how much they had missed at this first crime scene. She had a sick feeling in her gut about what they were going to find. In her mind, she began singing the death song, wishing that she was alone and not in front of a white FBI agent.

Overhead, a hawk circled occasionally, calling out an eerie high-pitched cry. Tom and Tally watched the hawk and trembled, both moving away from Gryffin and chanting and singing sotto voice, as they began to move to do what Gryffin had asked them to do. They knew everything was about to change and it was bad.

Chapter Seven

It was the body of a child. A small infant, wrapped in rabbit skin on a cradleboard, a thin rectangular board laced with leather laces. The face was perfectly formed, dark thick hair, eyes closed. The child had been dead for some time, and it was not possible to see the cause of death. There would have to be an autopsy. It was now 3:00 AM and Gryffin had been sitting beside the FBI Evidence Response Team Unit member excavating the body of the child.

This was not his normal job, but he had a deep intense feeling that every part of the ritual of these killings had meaning to their murderer. It had taken the Forensic Response Team three hours to get to the site and the team had lit up the interior of the pueblo and the exterior using large bar lights that heated the room. Other technicians were walking the grid again, clothed in PPE and armed with evidence bags and cameras. Gryffin knew the child predated the first body found here. It might have been the mitigating factor that began the killings.

Every few scoops of dirt were given over to another technician, who took it out to be screened to make sure no evidence was lost, and another photo was taken. Gryffin's shoulder hurt horribly. A wind had come up at sunset, chilling his body as it went across the floor of the valley. In the background, he could hear coyotes singing in the night.

His skin felt hot and yet he felt chills roll through his body over and over as they lay there. The investigator next to him cleared the last edge of the cradleboard and began to lift the body of the child out of the shallow grave. Gryffin continued to shoot pictures as they both inched back away from the pitiful hole and the body was carried out the door of the pueblo.

Gryffin felt more than saw the presence of a crowd, although it was pitch dark beyond the lighted area. On the hills above them, drums began and on the wind the sound of chanting or maybe singing began to float down to them. The wind was scented with burning sage and cedar. They quickly placed the baby on a gurney with a body bag, so pitifully small, and zipped up the sides pushing the gurney into the van as soon as it was done. Gryffin rolled his shoulders, trying to ease the pain.

He also felt another presence. It felt malevolent. He tried to resist the urge to look around but couldn't help look over at Tom. Behind Tom, he thought he saw two small red eyes not far away. '*Must be an animal*,' his logical mind stated to him, but he shivered nonetheless. He closed his eyes and pinched the bridge of his nose. He felt dizzy and tried to get his body to work beyond his fatigue.

Gryffin took the memory card out of the camera and passed it to the ERTU technician and began to pack up his gear. He looked at Tom, standing ghostly and white on the edge of the crime scene lights, suddenly feeling anxious. Tom's face was passive, but his eyes reflected the horror of the scene and maybe even guilt that another body had been missed. He handed the camera bag to Tom and asked him to put it in the Rover. Then he walked over to the ERTU scene supervisor and spoke to him so that no one could hear what he said. The Hopi Police Chief, Saufkie, was standing next to Detective Talayumptewa, and he went to them next.

"They'll be here for another three or four hours. I've made arrangements for someone to stay here guarding the crime scene. I've briefed them on appropriate and respectful behaviour. I'll make sure all reports go to your email. Any crime scene photos. Chief Saufkie, we are going to have to go over the other sites just as thoroughly. Tomorrow I'll send a new team to site two, at 10:00 AM if you or Detective Talayumptewa want to be there or if you want one of your deputies on the scene while we investigate. If you want me to have face time with the council, I can."

Chief Saufkie shook his head. "Let's get this over. It's Federal now and our hands are tied. If we can have one of us on site, we will. I'm short-staffed."

"I understand. I just want to make sure we are respectful and comply with as many of your requests as possible."

Saufkie looked into Gryffin's face and nodded. "I appreciate your respect for our customs. You're an unusual man for…" his voice trailed off.

"An FBI agent?"

Chief Saufkie smiled.

"You should be careful, Agent Gryffin." He tapped the medicine bag around Gryffin's neck.

"Don't take that off. No matter what goes on."

Gryffin looked at Saufkie's face. He was very serious, and he too looked as if he was grieving. Gryffin nodded before speaking again, "I would like to set up space at the Council

Chambers, but I need to know that it will be a secure room. If not, we can bring a van in to use as a headquarters. It's up to you, you do not need to decide right now. Morning is enough."

"I will be the coordinator for all efforts of this investigation," Gryffin continued, "and everything will go through me, and I will pass it on to you in real-time if I am able. We do not want to step on anybody's toes, and we want to be respectful of the Hopi Nation. But we can't have another scene not completely investigated and we want to stop this. We want to catch him."

There was a flash of anger in Chief Saufkie's eyes that passed quickly. He nodded.

Gryffin stopped and scrubbed a hand across his face, trying to still the pain in his head and in his shoulder. "Is there anything you need from me before I go?" Gryffin asked.

Chief Saufkie looked beyond Gryffin to the van. "How long until the child is returned to us?"

Gryffin shook his head. "I'm sorry. At this point I have no idea… they'll have to do an autopsy." Chief Saufkie began to look unhappy, and Gryffin quickly said, "We have to try and identify the parent or parents, unless you suspect someone you know? Or someone has reported a missing child?"

Saufkie stared hard and then shook his head.

"We'll do as much as possible to not be invasive. However, we need to know if this is our original killer or… someone else." The Chief's face never changed, but his eyes look sad and aged beyond his years. After a moment, he nodded.

"Quicker is better, Agent Gryffin. This is bad for all of us. The way *He* is handling the dead. It's very bad."

"I appreciate your concern. I will do my best to work this case. But from here on out, no more secrets. If we're going to resolve this, I need your full cooperation. And this will be on the Federal Governments' dime, not the Hopi. I believe you've lost enough." Gryffin ran his hand over his face again, trying to stay focused. His head felt like it was splitting, his shoulder throbbed, and he was suffering from vertigo.

Chief Saufkie nodded. "We're a small force. There isn't much money and it's a small community. Each city has its own leaders, so there are a lot of... opinions. But we are a loving, close-knit, spiritual community. This is devastating for all of us. It will take a long time to heal from this."

Gryffin nodded. "I am sorry for all the loss your community is dealing with. Our people will be sensitive to your community's needs. I'm going back to FBI headquarters and then I'll go to the hotel from there. I've got to get some more material and arrange for more help. The quicker we get in and out, the better off we all will be."

Chief Saufkie looked out into the darkness. He took a large breath and let it out. "Take care Agent Gryffin." He walked back to Deputy Talayumptewa.

Gryffin stared after him for a moment and then moved over to Tom.

"I've called for a helicopter. It'll take me back to the hotel. I've got to get some sleep and then I'll meet you at the second murder site. The ERTU unit will finish here and then a second unit is coming and will meet you at the second site. I've got a lot of notes to make. I want to let the units work without hindrance. No one, and I mean no one gets within a hundred feet of any of the sites. If you haven't done so already, put an agent at each site until the ERTU has cleared them. We will go in order. If you have problems, let me know. To make it official, I'm getting subpoenas to release each site to us so Chief Saufkie doesn't have to take any grief from the council. I want an incident van at the council headquarters by morning. Make sure everybody keeps their mouth shut and an eye on all the sites, all the time. At daylight, if anyone is still hanging around, and I mean above or below, I need you to take pictures of the crowd."

Tom began to object but Gryffin cut him off.

"You have a serial killer who is highly ritualised." His voice was razor-sharp. "We already know he returns to the scene. I don't care if you use a body cam, but we need to get ahead of this. Then you and I need to sit down and talk. You've had four serial killings, and this is a major fuck up." He paused to let that sink in. "I should have been called in two murders ago, especially since the delicacy of this situation with the Hopi Nation and the Federal government. The repercussions of this are going to go on for years. We are about to walk over the Hopi people to get this guy, disregarding their customs and people are going to be angry and vocal."

"The Navajo are going to be involved too," Tom said quietly. "These cross some of the borders."

Gryffin nodded. "Coordinate with Navajo Tribal Police. I'll take a helicopter to the second site. I'll see you there."

A helicopter sat warming up further down the valley, its boundaries marked by flares. Gryffin turned and walked down the dirt road to it. He felt the weight of the world on his shoulders, he could also feel eyes staring after him as he walked. Suddenly, an owl flew down in front of him, so close he could feel the brush of a wing against his cheek, and he ducked. He stumbled on the road and went down on one knee.

From behind him, he heard Tom running down the hill toward him.

"Gryffin, you, OK?" Tom's eyes were wide, and he was clearly spooked. He got to Gryffin and grabbed his arm to help him to his feet. Gryffin brushed at the dirt on his pants and glanced back to see Chief Saufkie's stricken face.

"Yeah, I'm OK. That was a little too close. What was that? An owl? It was huge."

Tom shifted nervously. "Yeah. An owl."

Tom swallowed and then said, "As portents go, they couldn't get much worse."

Gryffin looked at him startled. "Why?"

Tom scuffed his boot in the dust. "An owl is a bad omen. It's the sign of a witch. Or death."

"How appropriate…" Gryffin muttered. He turned back and continued down the hill to the waiting helicopter. Before he climbed in, he made a point of stomping his feet, shaking the dust off his boots.

Chapter Eight

Mary pushed a red curl of hair back behind her ear and smiled up at the fan in front of her. She looked back down and finished autographing the book and passed it back. The next fan stepped up and she smiled and reached for the book, not really paying attention. "Who shall I make it out to?"

"Ima Khoroshen'kiy. I-m-a, K-h-o-r-s-h-e-n-k-i-y."

Mary thoughtfully wrote the name in the book, as she handed it back and looked into the face of a Doppelganger. Startled, Mary froze for a moment and the book dropped from her hand. The young woman smiled at her; her eyes unnaturally green. The smile was so fake and so threatening, Mary shivered involuntarily and the two security guards behind her leaned in a little. She took a deep breath and shook her head slightly. The woman winked at her, picked up the book and stepped away into the crowd.

Mary turned her head back to one of the security guards, (she had jokingly named them Thing One and Thing Two). "I need a little juice."

Immediately Thing One handed her juice. She unscrewed the top and drank about half of the bottle. She was having a weird out-of-body experience after seeing the face of someone who looked exactly like her, and she was shaking a little. It had been like looking into a mirror. It made her feel uncomfortable, and she had learned from experience to trust that feeling. Her eyes scanned the crowd of smiling, eager fans. She must just be feeling paranoid. Mary could see there was no threat here. She looked up and motioned for the next person in line to step up.

Mary rolled her shoulders and kept going. She had another hour before a short break and a trip to another local bookstore. She missed Hege. She missed her brother Rick. She missed… she felt a shimmer of longing and need pass through her. A physical need for him. For Gryffin. She tried to slow her breathing, but the memory of their love making before he had left her on the ship came back to her vividly. She knew her face was growing red. While waiting to take a selfie with a fan, she waved her hand in front of her face to cool herself down. This was not a good place to go to mentally. She tried to switch gears. She had to continue to focus on work.

The last night she had watched TV and seen a blurb about an investigation on the Hopi Reservation. There was a media blackout, and the reporters were complaining about how tight the FBI and the Chief of Police were being. It was beautiful and sunny, and in the background behind an FBI spokesperson she had caught a glimpse of dark hair on a tall man, dressed in PPE, his back turned to the camera, but she knew it was him. Gryffin. She had felt an intense longing for him just like she was feeling now. This was tougher than she thought. They both were professionals; both had work to do. All she wanted was to hear his voice.

Mary turned back to Thing Two and said, "Potty break." She stood and looked out at the people still in line. "I'll be right back." She walked back with Thing Two in the lead and

Thing One trailing her to the back of the store. There was a women's bathroom there. Thing Two opened the door and called out to see if anyone was in the bathroom. There wasn't an answer. So, Thing Two went into the bathroom, opened stall doors and cleared the room. Thing Two came out and looked at Mary.

"All clear."

"All righty then," Mary said. She really didn't feel the need to use the restroom. She just needed a break out of the sightlines of everyone. She slipped the burner phone out of her pocket and stroked the case, thinking of Gryffin. She turned the camera on and sent a saucy picture to him. You couldn't see her face; her red hair was hanging in front covering everything. But her green eyes could just be seen. She smiled to herself and hugged the phone thinking of the look on his face and imagined being with him.

Chapter Nine

In his pocket, the burner phone vibrated. He knew it was from Mary. He wanted to pull the phone out immediately but he was standing along the wall in a meeting at the Flagstaff office of the FBI. Three of the crime scenes were pictured on three white boards. Three different Kachina's represented. Warrior Maiden or *He-e-e* or *He-Wuhti*, Maiden Spirit, or *Ahold Mana*, and Butterfly Maiden or *Palhik Mana*. Different aspects of the ERTU team were in going over the forensics, no clear prints, no discernible DNA. Each body's feet and hands were skinned. Each one raped and beaten to death. Their faces almost obliterated. Bodies washed of any evidence. Gloves worn. The body of the baby was the only anomaly.

The baby had made Gryffin feel angry and sad. The infant was a newborn, small and early. In the first few X-rays, it was evident the lungs had never expanded. Stillborn. But why buried there? DNA was still being run. No known birth had happened where a baby had been stillborn. No one reported it either. Teenager more than likely. Hidden pregnancy? But why bury the baby there? Was it part of the previous crime scene?

They were still trying to determine how long ago the baby had been buried. From the primary crime scene photos, you couldn't determine if the wood had been stacked. There were almost five weeks from the first murder, so the baby was born and buried before then.

Gryffin shifted as the phone vibrated again. He had finally woken that morning with the absence of a migraine, but the medicine he was taking made his mouth dry and his eyes itch. He scanned the room one more time and then his eyes landed on Tom Evehema. Tom at least had the good sense to look chagrined.

Two days previously, in a sit-down meeting with Tom in a room at the Flagstaff office, he had grilled Tom for two hours.

"Look," said Tom for the fifth time. "The Hopi are very spiritual people. When somebody dies inside a home, we abandon the home. Our belief system says their ghost may stay at the pueblo and any spirits that are attracted to the dead can still hang out. That's why the Hopi don't go into places after dead people are gone. They abandon the home. That's as ingrained in us as breathing is to you."

Tom continued, "As far as they are concerned, I'm a ghost to the Hopi. I left to become a marine and then was recruited from the Corp right into the FBI. The Hopi feel I am not a Hopi anymore. I went to the dark side. You can't be ignorant of how Native Americans feel about the Federal Government. I was supposed to make a path for a free exchange of information and to specifically aid the needs of the reservation and any criminal investigations that would fall into our jurisdiction. But they won't look at me or even speak to me directly. I'm a goddamned red apple to them! The old people

54

believe only a ghost, or a demon would work for the Feds and come back on the Res looking like somebody who left. My presence there is an embarrassment to the Fed's and to my tribe."

"And Tally…" he ran a hand through his hair in exasperation.

"I grew up with Tally. We went to school together. We dated until I went into the Corp. No, I didn't handle it well and there's some history there. At least she'll speak to me, of course without looking at me, but… you know what I'm saying, I'm trying for a professional relationship. OK, mostly I'm failing at communication but…" he just stopped talking as he looked at Gryffin's countenance.

Gryffin's face was stern.

"So, the next few weeks or months… you need to set aside that part of your Hopi heritage that is keeping you from doing your job unless it directly pertains to the crime scene, our perp or the people involved. For today and the following days, you are an FBI agent. And I need that trained professional working beside me every day. This is a dangerous perpetrator. These scenes are highly organised and thought out. This guy is meticulous. To catch him we are going to need a break, a big break. He isn't going to devolve unless something happens. He's in control, and he is not done."

"You can learn a lot here, or you can't. But you have to compartmentalise. Whatever you have to do, you do it. After the meeting tomorrow, do your interviews at Tribal Police Headquarters or at the FBI incident van. I think they'll feel more comfortable at the Tribal Police Headquarters, but you get them done in record time. Be sensitive, but get the information we need."

Gryffin paused before saying, "We're going to the last site and when we're done, you'll start interviews with the limited number of witnesses and family members, and you are going to do each one. I want them videotaped. Make peace with it after we get this guy. Do we have an understanding?"

Tom nodded. He had dark circles under his eyes: a clear sign that he hadn't slept either. Since Gryffin had arrived it had been one giant nightmare for him and for his tribe. But if he was being fair, the nightmare began with the murders. The Hopi were not prepared to deal with this kind of evil.

The meeting was coming to a close when the Special Agent in Charge, Mike Dubrowski, turned to Gryffin and asked, "Anything to add, Gryffin?"

Gryffin pushed off the wall and looked around the room. "I don't need to remind you to tread carefully on this. Make sure that if you are at a scene, talking to a witness, or just looking around, make sure you are 'sensitive'…" a huge groan went up in the room. "Yeah, I expect you all to go over the memo I sent you with guidelines for the behaviour and methodology of dealing with the Hopi. Today we are going to the last scene, which is on the border of Hopi and Navajo land. Land that is in dispute and is wrapped up in Federal court. I have no idea what's going to happen, except this. We are professionals. We stand firm, and if not, I have a pocket full of subpoenas to hand out. Regardless, we'll all maintain a level of professional integrity and behaviour that no one, and I mean no one can come back on the FBI. The first man or woman who crosses the stupidity barrier will be working in Alaska before the week is out. Clear?"

There was general grumbling, but heads nodded, and people started heading out of the meeting. "Tom, let's go. I'll meet you on the helipad in five minutes." Gryffin's burner vibrated in his pocket again and he headed for the men's room. Checking the stalls, he went to the last one and closed the door before removing the phone from his pocket. He opened the message and saw a picture of Mary signing books. She was smiling into the camera. He stood, looking at it for a moment, smiling, when something bothered him about it. It had come from a blocked number. When he looked at the past messages, he saw what was off.

Someone else had sent him the picture.

Chapter Ten

Skinwalker lay quietly at the edge of the mesa. He wore buckskins the colour of the dirt, sagebrush on either side of his body masking it from the sky. Over his shoulders, he wore the skin of a wolf. The sun was just reaching the zenith and he sweated through his shirt. He had silently watched the helicopter deliver the two FBI agents to the site. It was overrun with ERTU and people in PPE, looking bleached white in the sun. He wasn't worried about the FBI. He felt that he had perfected his method the way he had been taught. This wasn't a disadvantage. This was a challenge. Just as his mentor had taught him. His father had left him unprepared and directionless. His mentor had come at a time he was ready to begin. His mentor helped him focus and to be clean in his methods and preparation.

He thought of his father, the Navajo who had taught him to be a *Brujo*. It was in their blood for hundreds of years. His father had taught him brutal lessons. His father had washed away his Hopi mother's blood from him over and over. And then trained him to become a Skinwalker. To become one, his final task was that he had to kill someone at the age of sixteen and then he was transformed.

He had already begun his plans for the next *Kachina.* He knew the Hopi were afraid. The talk in the villages was already full of fear. People went in groups between their homes. Whispering gossip floated through the mesas. It made him hard to think they wouldn't say his name.

Some would suspect him, but he had been so cautious with the Navajo. He was a respected member of the community, carrying on in his artist father's footsteps. The family shop sold his *Katsinas* carved in the Hopi style. He also made *Kachinas* in the Navajo style.

He wanted to stand up and scream from his high perch. He wanted to wield a spear and call out to the gods in the sky above his head and sing a war song. He wanted to obliterate the white man. He wanted to bury all the Hopi who had killed his mother. He wanted to sing Navajo songs in front of all the pueblos until they crumbled to dust, and the Navajo would have all the Hopi land.

Time. He had time. Rushing was the path to destruction. If not today, tomorrow. Waiting. A hunter waited. Patiently waited. Perfection in the kill and the craft was the objective. He sat watching them for an hour more and then wriggled back from the edge so as not to raise any dust. He finally came up on his knees and then turned and duck-walked down the back of the bluff he was on until he could stand and not be seen.

As he moved through the cactus and down into the gulley, he felt the ghost of a smile race across his features. When he got to his truck, he pulled the sage covering it and threw it to the side. He climbed in and turned the key. Nothing. Then he tried again and again. On the third try, the engine turned on and he slowly rolled out on the washed-out road, leaving the barest of dirt clouds behind him.

He began to sing and chant as he drove, the air carrying his song across the desert.

Chapter Eleven

Mary's burner vibrated. She was in the back seat of the town car moving on to her next stop. She took the phone out, keeping it covered with her hand, so her driver didn't see what she was looking at. It was a picture of Gryffin in white PPE in the desert, the dirt dark red showing amid many other people. The smile froze on her face as she realised Gryffin didn't take this picture. The number was blocked and the photos were different than their usual way of communicating.

Her work cell phone rang. She slipped the burner into her pocket and pulled out the work phone and saw that it was Gryffin's old cell. She answered the call but did not speak.

"The phone's tapped," he said, then he hung up.

Mary leaned forward to the driver.

"I think we have a problem."

The driver looked at her in the rear-view mirror. He immediately turned right at the next corner, pulled to a stop, and began speaking into his handheld.

Mary looked out the window, trying not to worry that Gryffin's life may be in danger because of her. She was powerless.

Chapter Twelve

Gryffin had placed a call to Mary's current head of security, who met Mary at her next signing and asked for the burner. He immediately removed the chip from the phone and disabled it. He walked away from Mary without a word, and Mary went back to work with twice the number of security people surrounding her. Mary shuddered and thought about how she missed Gryffin's calm presence. She missed Hege even more. She made a mental note to 'casually call' Hege to see when she was coming back. She didn't want to pressure her at all. Hege was very astute. She'd quickly see through any pretence Mary displayed. She should probably just be straight up about it. She turned to the crowd and smiled and waved.

Mary greeted the store owner and shook hands, not really hearing anything that was being said. She felt a flicker of her past panic attacks edging up on her. She took a deep breath, then sat down and went to work. Time blurred as two more hours passed and she was done for the day and back to the hotel. She was making mental notes about her next steps and made a decision. She continued to smile, take pictures, sign books and when she left, she gave the manager an extra 200 signed book plates to use for their store.

Mary noted she had two more security guards with her, hustling her to the waiting town car. She slid into the seat and there was Hege, looking straight ahead. Mary reached over and hugged her. Hege patted her arm.

"I'm so glad you're back. You are back, aren't you?"

Hege turned toward her and Mary's eyes widened at the four-inch scar that ran along Hege's beautiful jaw line. Hege nodded. Mary could see that Hege had lost weight and looked pale. But otherwise, she looked like the Hege she knew. Mary faced forward and realised there were tears coming down her cheeks. She brushed them away with the back of her hand.

Hege turned to look at her. "Are you OK?"

"Yes." Mary cleared her throat. "I guess I just missed you."

Hege handed Mary another phone. It started ringing the minute she put it in her hands. Mary answered.

"Mary?" it was Gryffin's worried voice.

She hesitated a minute, too choked up to answer.

"Mary? Are you there?"

"Yes, Gryff…" she sobbed, suddenly overwhelmed.

"What's wrong? Are you OK?"

"Yes," she said sniffing. "Hege's back."

"I know. I called her as soon as I realised we had been hacked. Are you really, OK?"

"Yes. Just emotional I guess."

"You're suffering from PTSD. Take a couple of deep breaths."

"OK." She did what she had been told. " I miss you."

"I know sweetheart. Believe me, I'd be with you if I could. Hege is the next best thing."

"Where are you?"

63

"I'm at a crime scene. It's pretty tense here. Baby, I've got to go. Trust Hege. I'll speak to you tonight. May be late."

"I don't care. Whenever." She paused. "Gryff…"

"I know. Me too."

And the line went dead. Mary sighed heavily, cradling the phone against her chest. Hege looked at her again and Mary just shook her head.

"I'm OK. Thank you for the phone. Did you figure out who hacked us?"

"No. I have a team checking out Gryffin's room at the hotel and then I'm going to move him and put a team on him."

"Are you going to tell him?"

"Yes," she smiled at Mary, "and no."

Mary smiled back. "Have there been any new threats?"

Hege frowned. "Not directly. But this is."

She gestured at the phone.

"Gryffin has already contacted the FBI in Seattle but there isn't anything new. This feels familiar or at least similar."

"There was a woman at the signing. It was really weird. She looked just like me." Mary glanced directly at Hege and shivered.

"I mean everything, eyes, hair, face… it was like looking in a mirror. And I… she winked at me when she left. It was really creepy."

"Yes, I got the feed from the team. I'll get more information on her from the face recognition. It takes a little bit."

"Face recognition. Dang."

A smile flittered across Hege's face.

"Yeah, I have a guy."

"You have a guy. No doubt,"

Mary chuckled and then reached for a tissue from the box sitting on the seat beside her. She blew her nose and wiped her cheeks. She leaned her head back against the seat. "Is he safe?" her voice barely audible.

Hege hesitated before answering. "No. I'm not going to lie to you. The Res is a difficult place to be in as a white man. But a federal officer? This is a bad killer. The dark net is calling him 'Skinwalker'."

"Skinwalker? That sounds ominous."

"This is a *real* bad guy. He has a presence on the dark net, or did. Now he's not on it at all. But he was. It's impossible to back hack these guys. They float in and out of these chat rooms."

"You're tracking him."

Hege didn't say anything for a moment, "I'm always tracking these guys."

Mary looked forward, closed her eyes and shivered again, sending a quick prayer for Gryffin's safety and hers.

Chapter Thirteen

Gryffin put the new phone in his pocket and turned back to the scene. He could feel the eyes of someone or something boring into his back. He rolled his shoulders and for the hundredth time turned his back to the scene and looked at the surrounding mesas. At the top of the one directly across, there was an open space between two sagebrush. Before he could swear, it had been filled. He allowed the noise from the group of Navajo protestors who had come at dawn to stand at the scene shouting and name-calling to wash over him. Never really crossing the border, they stood in the dust at the edge of the tape and made noise.

Gryffin heard a hawk crying and he looked up into the sky, shading his eyes despite the dark glasses to see the wingspan of a red-tailed hawk floating in the air currents over the scene. Unconsciously, he reached for the amulet and his medicine bag, his index finger stroking across the hawk fetish.

An hour later, a group of Hopi stood outside the crime scene tape on the other side, quietly watching the ERTU team and the Navajo. Deputy Talayumptewa and SSA Tom Evehema stood in front of the Hopi line, both stone faced and observing the crowds. Gryffin felt as if he were on a tightrope. He reached up to the amulet around his neck again, realising he had gotten into the habit of touching it, and then praying, or whatever his version of praying was. Mary's face came into focus in his mind and a smile flitted across his face.

Tom watched Gryffin as he touched the medicine bag around his neck again. Although he felt no threat to himself, he had an unusual amount of anxiety about Gryffin. Tom reached into his pocket, affirming that his medicine bag was there. Tom also heard the hawk and glanced up to see it floating on the wind above them. He heard a truck trying to start. It was echoing off the canyon, and not in his line of sight. It took the truck three times to start.

Gryffin watched the last of the ERTU people coming out of the pueblo and carrying their gear to the truck. The scene's head tech walked over to Gryffin. Gryffin put his back to the Navajo line. "Did you look at the feet and hands? Was the skin gone?"

The tech nodded and Gryffin looked back over his shoulder at the crowd.

"Did you take crowd photos? You've got to be completely circumspect."

The tech nodded, headed back to the van and removed a camera. He moved to the side of the van and called to the other tech. He pretended like there was a problem with the camera. Gryffin walked to the line of Navajo people. He stood in front of them, scanning faces. They became silent and just stared at him. Then a few of the women began to hiss at him, and the men began to speak in Navajo, shaking their fists. Gryffin was pretty sure it wasn't a blessing. He memorised faces and then turned his back on them and walked back towards the van. Tom came towards Gryffin.

"You like living on the edge," He looked over Gryffin's shoulder and into the crowd of Navajo.

Gryffin just grunted, "Who's staying on site?"

Tom frowned. "I am. Tally hasn't slept in a couple of days. She'll sleep in the truck and then take over from me."

"How are you getting back? I'm taking the chopper when the ERTU leaves. I have some research coming in and I have to go over it at the office," He looked at Tom's stern face. "How are relations with the Hopi? And more importantly, how are you?"

Tom turned to look back at the Hopi protestors, none of whom would look at him directly, "Mostly just keeping an eye out. They are not happy. But Chief Saufkie is keeping them apprised and has explained to them the 'financial' implications of the FBI paying for all this. What little they did do almost wiped out what budget they had," He paused for a moment. "I'm tired, but…" he looked back at Gryffin and said softly, "By the way, I found a roll of film at the police station."

Gryffin looked at him. "Honest-to-God film from a camera?"

Tom smiled a lopsided grin, "Yeah. I couldn't be sure when it was shot or who did it, but I pocketed it and I sent it to headquarters to get it developed and to digitise it. It can't be used as evidence because there is no trail, no date, no ID, or who shot it."

Gryffin frowned, "Are you sure it was from our crime scenes?"

"No, but I thought that it might shed some light. And I can't be sure that it wasn't left out for me to take…"

"Why is that?"

"Not there one minute, there in front of me the next. I'm pretty sure whatever is on there, they want us to see it."

Gryffin scrubbed a hand across his face. He felt the beginning of another migraine coming on. He looked up and got a thumbs-up from the ERTU team. "OK. I'm out of here." He pulled his company phone from his pocket and contacted the helicopter pilot on the line. "I'm ready," he said into the phone and hung up. Unconsciously, he lifted his hand to the medicine bag and held on to it for a moment.

Tom saw him touch the amulet and then watched him walk away. He called after him, "Hey, Gryffin, wait."

Gryffin turned as a rifle shot cracked and echoed through the canyon. Gryffin felt the bullet graze his shoulder and dropped to the ground. He heard screams and could see that both lines of protesters had scattered and flattened themselves on the ground, heads covered. The ERTU team was under the van. Tom was kneeling on top of Gryffin with his weapon drawn. He never even heard Tom run up on him. Gryffin tapped Tom's knee and got up with Tom covering him. They got behind the van, scanning the mesas above them. There was silence. There was only the dust blowing in the wind. Even the hawk had vanished. Blood ran down Gryffin's sleeve and dripped onto the dirt, making a pattern.

Chapter Fourteen

Hege looked at the screen one more time and shook her head.

"The facial recognition is showing the woman as Mary. It's identifying her as Mary," said her contact on the other end of the line.

"So, they used plastic surgery? Use a woman with the basic same bone structure and then cut her to look like Mary? Who has the skill to do that?"

"Maybe three, or four plastic surgeons in the US. They can use some makeup and or formed masks, but the software is getting better and better to recognise any enhancements. This is some next level shit."

"No doubt. Send me the email. And be careful. I don't know what we're dealing with here."

"Roger that."

Hege frowned at the screen. Purpose? For what purpose? Was Mary replaceable? Was Mary important and was this a surrogate? Was this the same guy or some other perverse idiot? Nothing to do about it now. She filed it away in a part of her brain.

'*Compartmentalise.*'

Chapter Fifteen

Six hours later, Gryffin was finally climbing into his chopper, still remembering the ritual of stamping the dirt from his boots. He was bone tired and had a raging migraine… He'd used his injectable pen when the ERTU team looked at his shoulder on the scene. He'd also taken both oral medications for his migraine. The sun still cut through his dark glasses until he felt he was nearly blind from the light. He had felt that bullet coming, but it was only because he had turned at the moment the shot was fired that he was alive. He'd have to start wearing a vest.

Gryffin told Tally and Tom they should both have vests and that anyone covering the crime scenes needed to wear one too. Tally told him no one in the Hopi Police Force could afford vests. Gryffin got on the phone to Hege, and she arranged vests to be delivered to Chief Saufkie and more coming out to the sites with vests for Tally and the other two deputies.

Gryffin put it out to the FBI that ERTU or anyone working the sites had to be wearing a vest if they were outside, and then corrected himself to say anyone working on the Res should be wearing a vest. They had recovered only a piece of the rifle bullet. It looked like 30-06, but ERTU wanted to take

71

it back to the lab to look at it. The site was processed and then shut down again. The ERTU team left at the same time Gryffin went to the chopper. He gave stern instructions to Tom to be on the lookout for any trouble and also told him if he or Tally were too tired, he'd get more FBI to cover the sites.

Gryffin knew at some point, the finances of this operation were going to catch up with him, but there were major players in this from the FBI standpoint and also the Hopi and Navajo Nations. Everybody was watching this hoping only good would come from it. He also was worried that something more would happen. To him the perp was just messing with them. He had also called to put a rush on the roll of film Tom had sent in.

Watching the landscape below as the chopper flew, he was once again struck by its beauty and isolation. He was also watching for any trucks or vehicles that were in the area. Most of the protestors had disappeared after the shooting, driving off in clouds of dust across the desert floor. He wasn't sure if they would show up again tomorrow or whether they felt they had made their presence known. There was a lot of anger around these killings. The media was dogging everyone and there were plenty of opinions being expressed by the native community about the federal government and anybody with two cents of an opinion, but they wouldn't say the names of the victims, or what had happened to them. It was a generally voiced indictment of the FBI. The media were after the local police, and they were looking as if they were staking out the FBI office in Flagstaff.

His mind wandered and he wondered where Mary was. He was also very grateful that she was back under Hege's

72

watchful eye. Hege's guys were good, but Hege was scary good.

He rested his head back against the seat, the noise from the helicopter magnifying his headache and making him nauseous. He began some deep breathing and allowed himself a little time to remember his time with Mary. He knew that they were very close and very new. But he could only think about the feeling of her being in his arms. How she responded to his every touch, every little sigh and breath. She was funny and quick-witted. He liked the fact that she wrote romance novels that were steamy and impractical. In the same moment, he realised that she would never have a normal life. The fans, the work, the threats…

Who had hacked them? He frowned. Who was smart enough to tap burner phones? He couldn't let this go for a moment. He made a mental note to talk to the techs back at Quantico. If he didn't get a break soon, with some actual sleep, he would drop. He started to doze and didn't wake until the chopper was setting down on top of the FBI office in Flagstaff. From the roof, he could see a crowd of people in front of the building. Keeping his head low, he got out of the chopper with his briefcase and crossed the roof to the access door. Waiting at the door was SSA in charge, Mike Dubrowski. He went to take Gryffin's briefcase, but Gryffin waived him off. They entered the building and then went to the elevator that would take them down to the offices.

"You, OK? We heard you were shot."

"Missed me by this much," he held up two fingers of his left hand, showing an inch in measurement. Mike took in his bloody shoulder and the dust on his clothes.

"Kissed the dirt, did you?"

Gryffin grimaced. "Just a light smack. But I'm feeling it. I have notes to do, then I'm going to turn in early. I'm waiting for some photos to come, if I can get those as soon as possible."

"Are those the ones from the camera roll?"

"Yes."

"Where'd those come from? No evidence tag, and nothing logged into evidence."

"Anonymous. But possibly relevant. We won't know until we see them. The Hopi police have little to no budget. I'm not surprised they would wait until the roll was finished before they let it be developed."

"Jesus. I know I don't have to say, 'Be careful,' right? This has landmine written all over it and I for one don't want my office thrown under the bus."

Gryffin looked at him. "I'm aware. I am doing the best I can with the mess this was in before I got here. I'm balancing your office, the Hopi and Navajo Nations and a serial killer and am doing the best I can."

"OK, OK. Don't get hot. I just meant, the building is surrounded by press and protestors. Be on your guard. The sooner we can close this down the better."

"Roger that."

The elevator doors opened, and Gryffin walked to his temporary office and unlocked the door. He set his briefcase on the desk and took off his bloodstained coat. His shoulder was burning, and he checked the bandage. He was tired and for once, set down the journal he had just picked up from habit, put it on his desk and made the decision to go back to the hotel, take a hot shower and get some sleep. He could come in early and work on his notes. He rolled his shoulders and tried to remember where he had parked the vehicle the FBI had given him. The new burner phone rang in his pocket. He pulled it out.

"We have a car waiting for you at the back door," And the caller rang off. He could swear that was Hege. He shrugged and decided to go with it. He put his coat on over his shoulder, put his brief case under the desk and left the office, locking the door. He rode the elevator down to the parking structure first floor and walked to the back gate. He walked into the bright sun and saw a black town car waiting just outside the gate. Hege stood leaning against the door of the car. She was smiling.

He shook his head and went through the guard gate and went to the town car. She opened the door for him. "Give me the jacket, I'll have it fixed."

"I have no doubt," he said, turned the coat over to her and climbed into the back seat and into Mary's embrace. The door quickly closed behind him and Hege climbed into the front seat. His eyes were closed, and her arms were around his neck. She bumped his shoulder and he unconsciously winced. Mary pulled back, tears in her eyes. "I'm so sorry. Are you hurt badly?"

"How in the world?" he asked looking into those green eyes.

"Hege has you under surveillance of course. I couldn't let you…" she started to tear up again and he just pulled her into his arms.

"I'm glad. I had such a headache, I didn't want to ask you to come because you have your own work to do, but God, I'm so glad you're here," He leaned back and took her face in his hands. He kissed her cheeks and then her lips and stayed for a long satisfying kiss. Her eyes were large and smoky. She looked at the bandage on his shoulder and lightly touched it. He caught her fingers and kissed the tips of them, "I'm OK. It was a graze."

"Awfully close." He paused and looked at her with curiosity.

"Did you see it?"

"It's all over the news. One of the protestors was filming with a hidden camera and caught the whole thing." She saw the look on his face. "I thought you knew…"

He sat back, closing his eyes. He scrubbed a hand over his face and then pulled out his work phone. "Mike. Protestor had a camera on us. You need to get a subpoena and pick it up from whatever news outlet has it. See if you can get a line on who filmed me. Yeah, I didn't know. I was on a chopper." He listened for a while.

"Yes, sooner than later. No, I'm not coming back until morning. I need some sleep and to get a stitch or two in my shoulder. Yeah. Yeah. Tomorrow. Bring whoever it is for an interview. Yes, I think it was a set up. OK. Tomorrow."

Mary was sitting back in the seat. "We moved your things…"

He looked over at her and smiled tiredly. He tucked an errant curl behind her ear. "Of course, you did."

She looked back at him and then leaned her head on his good shoulder and sighed heavily. "Am I more trouble than I'm worth?"

He kissed her head and pulled her in closer.

"No. Right now, at this moment, you are a godsend. You and my Danish fairy godmother, Hege."

Chapter Sixteen

He remembered sitting on the roof of the house, his feet dangling over the edge, so little a child he was. He was watching the dancers with his mother, sitting behind the elders, their heads wrapped with colourful scarves, their rattles in their hands with eagle feathers on them. They sang with the sound of the drums and bells ringing. The four dancers, in their costumes, wings of eagle feathers flapping like the flying eagle itself. He loved the colour of the red sash at their waists, the white kilts and the colourful masks they wore.

He could still hear his mother's voice in his ear, telling him what was happening in each part of the dance as the dancers hopped and stamped their feet in the intricate steps of the Eagle Dance. "Someday," she whispered into his ear. "Someday, you will be a dancer like them," chucking him under the chin. Her feet would bounce in imitation of the steps as they danced, and he would smile. He loved the song and the dancers. He loved the feel of her arms around him, safe and secure and yet so high up on the edge of the roof.

He woke from the dream, feeling her hand caressing his face. He sat up in bed, realising there were tears on his face. Angry with his mind and the thoughts that still betrayed him, he got up and took a cold shower, brutally scrubbing the Hopi blood out of his system the way his Navajo father had taught him.

Little Butterfly's face came to him so strongly he had to stop and lean his head and shoulders into the shower, shaking and quivering. He had taken her like his father had taken his mother. But she had not fought him. He thought she had welcomed him and when it was over, he had found himself being gentle with her. Her face was round, and she was very soft and plump like a bird.

He had visited her house many times at night, leaving trinkets and little presents for her on the doorstep of her house. Until his father had caught him. His father had followed him to Little Butterfly's house. He had known immediately what had happened. He had dragged him back across the Mesa behind a horse, his hands tied in front of him, stumbling and falling.

He had tried to find out about her. Tried to find out if she was all right. She was only fourteen at the time. Like a moth to a flame, he had not been able to stay away from her. And then he knew she was pregnant and felt an intense feeling of pride. He had found her struggling in birth, away from her family, in a deserted pueblo. The child being stillborn. Little Butterfly died a few hours later. He had taken the child and carefully washed its body, wrapped it in a rabbit skin, placed it on the cradleboard and carefully buried it in the dirt floor, covering it with wood from the caved-in roof.

He had hidden Little Butterfly's body from his father so that he could not desecrate her. He had hidden the child so that he could not defile it. It was why he had placed his first kill there. To honour Little Butterfly, although they would never know it or understand it.

They weren't meant to find the body of the child. It was the fault of the FBI agent. The FBI agent would have to pay dearly for disturbing the body of his child.

Chapter Seventeen

Tally woke with a start, lying in the back of Tom's Rover. His jacket and his definable musk was all over her. She was exhausted, still. She put a hand through her hair and then over her face. She'd had the dream again. When she was a little girl, maybe three or four, she had been playing in the bean field next to the corral with her mother's horses. It had been a lean year for rain and the dust was as dry as it could be, it was like powder on her little hands. Behind her, she heard the panting of a large animal.

Slowly, she turned to see the eyes of a mountain lion. Even as a child, she had frozen in place, not daring to move. The cat had been after the horses, but seeing easier prey, had focused on the child in the dirt. Little bits of her hair had come loose and floated in the wind around her face. She had been afraid for only a few moments.

In this remembering-dream, the fear rose in her and she grew from a child to a grown woman, still seated in the dust. The cat was steadily walking towards her, snarling. She knew it was the cat making the noise, but it sounded more and more like a man screaming and growling. Tally felt terror rise in her, heart pounding, her terror mounting. She couldn't call out, or scream. She could imagine the claws sinking into her flesh and tearing her apart.

Usually, in the dream, her mother would step in front of her. The cat would claw her mother's arm and then her mother would strike the cat in the face with her rifle and the cat would run away. But not in this dream. In this dream, the cat overcame her mother, knocked her to the ground, and then stood over her, tearing her body to shreds.

That was when Tally woke, in the back of Tom's Rover. She thought she might be sick, so she breathed in through her mouth for a few minutes. And then Tom was standing at the window.

"You, OK? I thought I heard you call out," he waited patiently. His face was a mask of concern.

"Bad dream. Really bad dream," she said shaking her head and tipping her face down so that he wouldn't see her tears.

"Oh, Tally…" was his only response.

Chapter Eighteen

As it was, Gryffin slept for 24 hours. When they got back to the hotel, they had moved into a suite. They had entered, hands clasped, at the back of the hotel through the kitchen with Hege leading and two security guards front and back, their hands on their weapons the whole time. Once in the suite, Hege stitched his shoulder herself with a mobile medic unit she always carried with her. Hege ordered food; meanwhile Mary and Gryffin showered, made love slowly and then came out to eat once everyone had left the main suite. Security was posted outside the door. Hege poured them wine and then left into the second bedroom off the main room, leaving the door cracked open a little.

After they finished dinner, they talked about Mary's last few days, future schedule and inconsequential things. Mary excused herself to freshen up. As if on cue, Hege came from her suite with some paperwork. She sat in a chair in the living room suite and Gryffin got up and sat on the couch opposite her. She laid some paperwork and photos down on the coffee table.

"Your room was bugged with some pretty high-tech devices. I still haven't figured out how they hacked the burners. Normally they would have to have them in their hands to add a bug or to clone them. The signal on the room monitor was going to the room next to yours. We have to assume he had a passkey. The room was wiped clean-no prints. He appears briefly on the camera from the hall when he came into your room as a room service steward. Never a clear shot of his face. I don't suppose you remember what he looked like?"

"Average. Nothing out of the ordinary. I was tired and had a migraine."

Hege looked at him critically. "You need some serious rest, or you will not be able to be any good to anyone. I'm leaving a team to follow you…" Gryffin lifted his hand to object, but Hege cut him off. "Before you say no, I think this is still about Mary and getting to her through you." She paused to let that sink in.

He closed his eyes and shook his head. "I agree."

"Have you had any overt threats that I can follow up on?"

"Other than being shot at?"

Hege gave one of her rare smiles.

"We both know that wasn't serious."

She frowned, thinking of something. "Although, it could come to be a problem. I already have someone on both reservations. So, we'll see what comes of that. I think it's someone else. Not your perp." She looked at his medicine bag that hung around his neck. "Where'd you get the amulet?"

"Hopi Shaman. I don't think it's working. You know," he said slowly, "at times you're a little scary."

"Yeah, yeah, I know. Mary's at the door." He turned around and Mary stood at the door to their room. She was wearing a diaphanous white negligee. "Good luck," Hege said under her breath and watched as Gryffin looked up at Mary, then rose and crossed the room to her like a moth to a flame. She opened the door wider for him and then closed it behind them.

He pressed her back into the door, kissing her until she was breathless. "You must have a very high opinion of me, Mary McKenzie. I haven't had five hours of sleep in three days, I've been shot, threatened, and spied on."

She giggled and began to rub against him, "Your body seems on autopilot. Once a marine, always a marine."

"Hoo-rah," he said lifting her and carrying her to the bed despite his shoulder injury.

Chapter Nineteen

Tom and Tally's phones rang at the same time. Tom had been sleeping in the back of the Rover and Tally had been on watch. He heard Tally answer almost as quickly as he said, "Agent Evehema."

The voice on the other end was short, stern, and direct. Another murder. Another body.

He sat up straight when he heard Tally's gasp of breath and her, "Oh no!"

He was out of the truck and running to her the second she collapsed to the ground, the phone dropped in the dust, her head bowed, her hair a black shining curtain in front of her face. She began to call out and scream.

He knelt behind her and very carefully took her into his arms. At first, it was as if she were a piece of wood, hard and unmoving. Then she relaxed her body into his, her right arm coming up to grab his arm in a hard grip of fear and anguish. She began to moan and cry as only she could do with him, the sound echoing off the canyon walls and scattering the birds from the brush.

The sun shone down on them; the air was so clean it hurt to breathe it in. The wind blew little dust devils around them, and he held her tighter, willing the world to stop, remembering everything they had meant to one another, every touch, taste and kiss. He felt the tremor of grief pass through her like an earthquake and he rode it with her, absorbing her grief and giving her the accepting strength of his own spirit.

Tom lowered his chin and kissed the top of her head and rocked her in his arms. Together they heard a truck coming down the hill toward them. He lifted her up until she could stand on her own, shielding her from the oncoming truck and then backed away from her, turning to face the Hopi as they came close to them in truck after truck.

Tally wiped her face with her sleeve and then turned to face her family, her village, her people who had come to care for her, with a passive and settled face: her grief roaring like the mountain in her mind and body.

Chapter Twenty

His phone was going off, and he lay on his stomach, his arm over the side of the bed. Gryffin felt better than he had for a week, and he could smell Mary's perfume on his pillow. He snagged his work phone off the nightstand and answered. "Hello?" his voice was gravelly, and he cleared his throat, got up on his elbows and said again, "Hello?"

"You still alive?" It was Tom.

"I'm downstairs and there's a chopper waiting on top of the Federal building. We've had another murder."

Gryffin sat up in bed. "Give me fifteen minutes."

"Don't forget your flak jacket."

"Never."

He was in and out of the shower noting that someone had set out a pair of jeans, boot socks and some mighty fancy snakeskin boots, along with a brand-new bullet-proof vest of high-tech Kevlar body armour. He had little doubt that everything would fit him like a glove. He smiled and suited up before leaving his room, hanging his badge around his neck and securing his Glock Gen 5 in the holster, heading to the elevator. He finished putting on his FBI-issued windbreaker leaving it open for the heat. Tom was waiting in the lobby and looked agitated and very distressed. He was about to speak when Agent Gryffin approached him, but Gryffin held up a hand and nodded toward the exit.

At the exit were protestors, which Gryffin simply waded through with Tom trailing after him and then catching up. The press was also waiting and followed them both to the yellow Rover. Gryffin didn't say a word and Tom drove through the crowd of protestors and reporters carefully and then got out on the boulevard and headed down to FBI headquarters. They went around to the back of the FBI facility, passing the guards and entering the underground parking. Tom was trying to keep up with Gryffin as he headed for the elevator and hit the buttons for the roof. Gryffin took a look at Tom and noticed he wasn't wearing his flak jacket.

"Where's your vest?"

"Oh, shit. I left it in the Rover. I'll go back and get it."

"Where's the latest?"

Tom took a ragged breath before answering.

"Again, on the border with the Navajo reservation. You think he's making a statement?"

"I think he's a psychotic serial killer."

The door opened on the floor Gryffin's office was on. Standing in the doorway was SSA Dubrowski.

"I need a quick word before you head off." Gryffin got off the elevator and Tom stayed on to go back and get his vest.

"What's up?"

"Two things. We got the guy with the hidden camera. Just a protestor. Nobody special, no connection," Dubrowski was frowning. "Those photos from the roll of film came back."

They walked down to Gryffin's office, and he unlocked the door. Gryffin picked up the file folder. "What am I looking at?"

"I think these are post-assault photos. Maybe domestic, maybe rape? They did some research and matched it up with Navajo police reports. The Navajo were the only tribal Police Force there. The Fed's had a force that worked the Hopi res."

The pictures showed a very young Hopi woman with multiple bruises and contusions to her face and body. In the photos she didn't look at the camera, her head was always downcast and looking away. The beating was horrific, and it looked as if she had bite marks on her breasts and neck. There were no identifying names, no dates on the photos. But on the back of the 8x10s there were dates marked. The last photos were of the same girl, but she looked about five years older, and she was clearly dead. The same pattern of abuse and attack was evident on her body along with the bite marks. A date five years later was marked on the back of the photo, but no name.

"Do we know the name of the girl?" Gryffin asked Dubrowski.

Dubrowski shook his head. "No. Name kept out of the report because the Hopi wanted to treat it internally. But ask Tom."

Gryffin looked at him and shook his head, "OK." Gryffin put the pictures back in the folder and put it in his briefcase. He felt Dubrowski's eyes on him. "What?"

"This is going to be bad, isn't it?"

"Yes. I'm thinking generational. Assault, abuse, rape."

"So Who's the assistant?"

"What?"

"Your assistant called to let us know you had to have recovery time and weren't to be disturbed unless it was an emergency."

A smile tugged at the corners of Gryffin's mouth, "Just an assistant," And with that, he left the office for the elevator and the roof of the building.

Once in the helicopter, Gryffin pulled out the photos and passed them to Tom. Tom's face turned white. He flipped through them a couple of times. He cleared his throat and then put the photos back in the folder. Gryffin thought he was stalling. He looked at Tom, his eyebrows raised, and Tom cleared his throat.

"Before my time. A Hopi girl, 14, raped. She was out riding, someone surprised her, or she met someone. Rumours both ways, that she was seeing a young Navaho buck," He paused and swallowed again. "She became pregnant from the rape and was hidden by her parents. They never let her go back to school. The child was a boy. When he was five…" he swallowed again, his features became saddened. "She was found, her body was found out on the mesa, raped, and strangled. I didn't know about the bite marks. I guess the police wanted to keep that quiet. The police at the time were Federal Government and Navajo Indian Police. They were not too concerned with prosecuting across Hopi/Navajo lines." He shook his head. "There were rumours."

"What kind of rumours?"

"The skin from her feet and hands was missing."

He looked out over the mesa, for quite a few minutes, then went on. "Two years later, the Hopi grandparents… they were raising the child… There was, were rumours about the child being mistreated. This is not something… I mean our traditions about raising children are very peaceful, loving… but this boy suffered. The grandparents died or were killed. There were rumours about what happened to them, but no

90

charges were filed. There was no other close family. No one would take the child in. And the child… went to the father, the rapist, the Navajo father, to be raised among the Navajo, as a Navajo."

Gryffin frowned and looked down, shaking his head.

"The problem is the child was no more welcomed by the Navajo than he was by the Hopi. We are very similar in background and culture, but also very different. This child had one foot in both worlds but was not accepted in either. There were rumours his father was a *Brujo*."

Gryffin's eyebrows rose, "A witch?"

"Yes. Look, both Hopi and Navajo people have a healthy belief in spirits, good and bad. It has only been in the last five years or so that the Hopi have revealed some of our deeper spiritual beliefs about being caretakers for the earth, and about our origin stories publicly. The Hopi are a deeply proud and spiritual people. We are gentle and respectful, and our beliefs and our culture are very important to us. The stories and oral traditions have been passed down for many generations and are a true part of who we really are. We do not share our spiritual beliefs with outsiders as a rule. They are sacred to us," Tom hesitated for a moment before going on.

"That's not to say, the Navajo are that much different. Medicine men and women in the Navajo traditions are taught both good and bad medicine. But they are taught the right way, the right path. Some… some choose a bad path. Corrupted by greed, or lust, or something else. Then they choose the witchery way. *Brujos*. But… the traditions of Brujos, and Skinwalkers…"

"Skinwalkers?"

"Listen, I know I'm an educated man," he paused to run his hand through his thick black hair. "I have been in the Corp, seen combat and war, and have trained with the FBI, but these customs, this lore, has its feet in truth and reality, you as a white man cannot comprehend. Every native American culture has a myth about shapeshifters. We believe to talk about them is to draw them to you or your family. Even just to say their names. Navajo believe they are men and sometimes women who change shape, slip their skins and become vicious, evil creatures. They can become wolves, coyotes, foxes, cougars, dogs, or bears. In Navajo, they are called *yee naaldlooshii*."

He paused and swallowed heavily, "This close, the Hopi, believe the same things. A *Brujo* becomes or calls a shapeshifter to him. A Skinwalker. They protect native land and native people. But this man has twisted it. He's harming not helping. In the light of day, most native Americans won't talk about or discuss these creatures with people outside our culture, even then... But in our heart of hearts, they exist. They are real to us. There are many parts of the reservation where these creatures have been seen, have been tracked, have been recorded. To acknowledge them is to bring them to your home, and we believe they can hurt us. They can kill people. They can make you sick or curse your land."

Gryffin had a faraway look in his eyes.

He refocused and looked at Tom.

"How does one become a Skinwalker?"

"They have to kill someone. Most times, a close family member."

"So, the belief is that the Navajo father is or was a Skinwalker? Or a witch? Or both?"

92

"The father is dead. And he **was** a *Brujo*. He was an artist making art for tourists."

"And the son?"

"Alive as far as I know. He makes... *Kachina* dolls for tourists like his father. He's a very well-known artist," Tom paused.

"And people believe he is a Skinwalker. It's why they won't speak his name out loud. They'll indirectly refer to him as the 'Doll Maker'."

"Tom. His name."

Tom drew a shaky breath. "His Hopi name was *Nuvakwahu*, Eagle. His father changed his name to a Navajo name. *Hashkeh Naabah*. Angry warrior."

Chapter Twenty-One

He sat in the sweat lodge he had created, a neat hole dug into the side of the arroyo, lined with rocks and green branches. A deep well dug and filled with charcoal made from cedar and sage created the smoke and a large hide over the entrance kept the fragrant smoke in. He sat in nothing but a loin cloth and breathed in the heat and the smoke allowing the peyote to work in his blood. He called to his ancestors in his mind, naming them and seeing their faces.

Purification and direction. Purification of body, mind, and soul. The sweat poured from his body making his limbs slick and heavy. He started to sway with the chanting and music that was in his head, falling back against the stone wall. Colours swirled and formed animals in his mind, and he felt them leaving his head. He watched as they danced around above his body. The wolf came and its huge head faced him. It's jaws were wide and slavering. The wolf was speaking to him, but he couldn't hear the words. He struggled to sit up to hear its voice.

His vision changed and he saw the eagle high above his head, floating on the currents of the air, the wind… he could feel the wind cooling his heated body. The cry of the eagle was his mother's cry, her scream and he struggled up from the dream until he was sitting up screaming. He scrambled out of the sweat lodge, crawling in the sand which covered his sweating body. The red sand looked like blood and he screamed again and again and again… just as he had as a child.

Chapter Twenty-Two

The new scene felt different. It wasn't in a pueblo but at the bend of a dirt road. The scene was set up similar to the other crime scenes, but this seemed a little more macabre. The corpse was completely covered in the *Kachina* costume although torn at the shoulder so that part of one arm was visible. This scene was exposed and there was a crowd around the scene. The first thing Gryffin did was make the ERTU unit put up shields and pop-ups over the body, virtually blocking the body from the crowd that surrounded it. The crowd was mixed this time. Chief Saufkie was there with Deputy Talayumptewa. Tom stayed with them talking quietly.

Gryffin stood in front of the *Kachina,* taking in its appearance. This *Kachina* was more elaborate. The doll was leaning against a rock and was sitting on top of a wolf's skin. Gryffin vaguely remembered this *Kachina* from his research days before. Although the name wouldn't come to him. This victim had nothing in her hands and wore a simple kilt with short leather boots. Over her shoulders was a brightly decorated shawl of wool. On her head, a simple mask, non-threatening, with long hair and the Hopi cut bangs. She had feathers on top of her head. And red knobs for ears. There was a piece of wood near her right foot.

Tally walked up beside Gryffin and began to speak in a low voice repeating what she had said at the first site. "*Katsinas* are Hopi. The Navajo are just carvers copying our spirits. But they cannot capture the essence of a Hopi *Katsina*. This is *Hahai'I Wuhti*. Grandmother or Pour Water Woman," Her voice sounded odd to Gryffin.

"*Katsinas* are made of cottonwood root?"

"Yes. He is accurate in the costume and the look. The stick on the ground is cottonwood. But this robs the spirit of the person he is killing to create his dolls," Her voice became hard for a moment, and he looked at her. "He is stealing souls. He is desecrating Hopi… he wants to end the Hopi, the whole tribe." She stood swaying slightly beside him, humming under her breath.

"Have you known any of the other victims?"

She swallowed hard before speaking again so softly, he was afraid he wouldn't be able to hear her, "We are a small, finite community. We know all the victims. By name. By clan. By family name. Hopi follow the matrilineal culture. So far each of the women were spirit women. What you would perceive as Medicine Women. They each had gifts… and he is trying to steal their power."

He turned to look at her. Her smooth skin was marred by deep circles under her eyes. Her hair was loose and hanging over her shoulders in dark glossy waves. Her uniform was unbuttoned a little and she wasn't wearing her utility belt. Had she been crying? "When was the last time you slept?"

"None of us are sleeping," she said, then closed her eyes and took a ragged breath.

"He comes when you sleep. First, he beats. Then he rapes. Then he murders. Then he desecrates. This is evil in its purest form. He is trying to destroy my people."

She moved away from him and went back to walk the line of protestors.

Gryffin wondered how they had come so quickly to the site. He walked to Tom and spoke to him so that he wasn't facing the crowd.

"Did you take crowd shots?"

Tom nodded silent and brooding.

"Who called this in?" Tom's eyes were unfocused and then he turned and looked Gryffin full in the face. His face was marked for the first time with emotion. He looked defeated and angry.

"Tally's uncle. Her mother was missing from their home…"

Gryffin stood shocked and was unable to draw breath for a moment. He looked to Tally and then back at Tom. "Have you identified her?"

Tom shook his head and his gaze wandered to Tally, standing straight but swaying slightly in the wind.

"Jesus, Tom. She can't be here. Did she touch anything?"

Tom's focus turned back to Gryffin. "No. She's been a consummate professional," he said harshly. Then he took a breath.

"There is a scar on her mother's right arm. The scar was made when she rescued Tally, a baby at the time, from a mountain lion." He was quiet for a moment.

"You won't be able to get her to leave. And all these people," Tom said, gesturing with his arm at the people gathered outside the perimeter marked by tape held down by rocks.

"They'll wait with her. She'll honour not touching the body or disturbing the scene. But… it's family and it's our traditions."

Gryffin nodded. He closed his eyes and felt a silent anger and sadness that was overwhelming in its scope. He reached for the amulet at his neck unconsciously, his hand squeezing the contents. Gryffin stood looking for a moment at Tally and then went back to the crime scene, making notes in his mind to write down later in his journal. His hand felt wet, and he wiped it on his dark jeans without thinking about it. He walked forward to stand in front of the body and then turned his back to the body to look at the surroundings. Dessert, mesas, cottonwood, scrub pine. Then he turned around quickly and looked at the placement of the body again. Crossroads. The body was placed at a crossroad. What message was he sending? A change? This was a change in location. What was different? Still a Hopi victim. Still near the ever-moving border of Hopi and Navajo land.

What was the significance of the crossroads? Gryffin was convinced this was an important part of his killer's process and that it was pointing in a direction. What direction? He cleared his mind, closed his eyes, and just listened. Suddenly the scene was quiet. The wind had picked up slightly. A storm cloud had come up over the mesa a tower of white and grey. He didn't know how long he had been standing there when he felt the first drop on his face.

The medicine bag felt heavy and slightly damp against his chest. He must have been sweating more than he usually did. He felt out of place and time and yet he still didn't move as the rain began in earnest. He didn't know how long he had been standing there but when he opened his eyes, he still didn't move but looked around, only turning his head. His vision was changing. Getting darker.

Tally stood apart from everyone, her hair unbound and loose, the wind and rain blowing it until it was plastered against her skin. Tom was a couple of feet away from her, soaked to the skin, with a look of such horror and pain in his eyes. The ERTU unit was putting up more plastic sheeting around the body to protect it from the rush of water suddenly pouring into the desert.

The drumming of the rain... it felt as if he heard another drumbeat. He felt as if the earth was shifting beneath his feet and the scene was actually spinning. He tasted blood in his mouth, though his head was actually light and empty of thought. He thought he was seeing shards of light coming from the cactus near him. Then he felt cold, as if he was falling, as if hands were touching him, pulling him down to the earth. His eyes rolled into the back of his head and his body shook as he fell onto the ground, the water from the rain pooling in his still open eyes, matting his dark hair, soaking his clothes.

There were voices shouting, yet he felt nothing but a buzz like bees from very far away. He never felt the hands that touched him. He fell into a dark abyss with the only sound being the drum.

Chapter Twenty-Three

Gryffin awoke inside an MRI machine whirring and thumping away. Everything was black. His head was restrained in the MRI cage, his hands were tied to the side of the bed of the MRI, and he was blind. He tasted bile in his mouth and tried not to panic. He closed his eyes and tried to even his breathing. "Mr. Gryffin? Are you awake?"

"Yes."

"We're almost through. Please don't move. Are you OK?"

He hesitated, "I'm blind."

Silence. "OK, sir. We'll get you through and back up to ICU as soon as we can."

He waited for what seemed a terribly long time, but they finished, and he felt cold, and a chill went over his body that set him to shivering. Gryffin couldn't move without being released from the restraints. He was starting to panic until he felt the presence of someone beside him, "Mr. Gryffin? My name is Jacob. I'll help you up, sir. Let me just remove the cage and the restraints."

"I'm blind. I can't see anything," Gryffin realised he was in a gown and his feet were bare. When he breathed in, he felt he could still smell sage and creosote from the desert. "OK, Mr. Gryffin, nice and easy," he felt a hand beneath his shoulder and a hand grasping his wrist. "Careful, sir. You have an IV. Let me move that. Can you sit up for me here, for just a moment?"

Gryffin nodded, feeling disoriented and dizzy. "I think I'm going to be sick to my stomach," he said suddenly, bile heavy in his throat.

"OK, OK. Let me get an emesis basin for you,"

He heard movement, trying to keep himself from vomiting. Someone lifted his hand and put a basin in it, which he immediately brought to his mouth and vomited. He spit a couple of times, and then someone took the basin and put a couple of tissues in his hand for him to wipe his mouth. "I've got a wheelchair here sir, do you think you can stand up for me?"

"I'll try," Gryffin stood up and wobbled a bit, the strong arm came back on his arm, steadying him.

"The wheelchair is a step in front of you," The hand pulled his arm forward to the arm of the wheelchair. Gryffin felt it and took a step forward, turned and awkwardly sat in the chair. "Here let me help you put your feet up." Gryffin hated the feeling of helplessness as the orderly put his feet onto the footrests of the wheelchair.

His anxiety rose, "I'm an FBI agent. Were my weapon and identification secured? How long was I out? Is this still…"

"It's Tuesday. I don't know anything about your things, I just picked you up from ICU, and there were a couple of 'federal' looking people, so I'm sure you're going to be fine. Try to relax."

Gryffin just nodded. He lifted his hand to his neck, realising his medicine bag was gone.

"I had an amulet on. It's not here."

"I'm sure it's with your personal items in your room. We can look for it when we get there."

"I'm blind. I can't see."

"When did this start?" Gryffin felt himself moving in the chair and began to feel nauseated again.

"Can you slow down a little? I'm very disoriented and nauseated."

"Sure. When did the blindness start?"

Gryffin hesitated. "Today, when I woke up in the MRI."

"I see," They rolled over an edge. "Just going to take a little ride on the elevator." Gryffin heard a button being pushed and heard the elevator doors close. He put his head down, trying to take even breaths so he wouldn't be sick again. He realised they were going down in the elevator. He lifted his head.

"I thought we were going *up* to the ICU?" Gryffin asked.

Whoever was near him chuckled. Gryffin smelled a heavy cologne that clogged his sinuses and made him gag. He heard some movement near his IV that was attached to the wheelchair.

"Clever boy. Too clever."

Suddenly the room spun heavily for Gryffin, and he cried out as if the whole earth was tipping, then utter blackness descended, and he was lost. Her name came to his lips in a whisper, a prayer crying out in his last moment of consciousness.

Chapter Twenty-Four

"Shouldn't he be back in the room by now?" Mary asked for what must have been the hundredth time. Hege patted her arm and walked down the hall to the nurse's station. The harassed ICU nurse liaison looked up as Hege approached.

"Sorry to bother you…" Hege began.

The nurse grimaced a smile and tapped a few buttons on the computer. A frown came cross her brow. "He was finished with the MRI 30 minutes ago. He should have been back in his room."

"Would they have taken him to his room another way?" Hege said, adrenaline dropping into her system with a rush.

"No. No. They have to come by me, there's no other access," Before the nurse could finish another thought, Hege was running back down the hall, talking into her handheld and stopping in front of the elevator. She banged the button a couple of times with her hand when the elevator opened. Mary had seen Hege rush by and had quickly followed after her.

When the elevator door opened, there was nothing but a wheelchair with an IV on the pole, a few drops of blood on the floor, a small amulet with a torn leather cord and the scent of a terrible cologne lingering. Mary took a deep breath, recognising the scent and screamed for all she was worth… Chaos ensued.

Chapter Twenty-Five

Tom Evehema was off his horse, checking his cinch, his face covered by a bandana to help him breathe in the wind that was blowing sand so hard it was difficult to see more than five or ten feet in front of him. Two days after a gully washing rain happened on this side of the mountains, a freak windstorm struck. He had made a decision to try and search the caves at Ghost Mountain. What he hadn't counted on was the windstorm that came after the pounding rain. People were talking in quiet tones about the weather and looking worried throughout the Res. He leaned into his horse and felt the camaraderie with this animal he had had since he was 24. The horse had been a gift from his grandfather, given when he got home from the Marine Corps.

His grandfather had told him to go out and try to remember the Hopi way of life and to shed the thoughts and beliefs of the white man. He had spent two months in the valleys and canyons, mesas and caves trying to decide whether he was going to take the job offered by the FBI. In the end, he wanted the job and he had taken it. The day he made the phone call to the FBI, his grandfather had passed. After the funeral, he had gone to Quantico. When he came back to the Res…

Tom began to have an affinity with Ghost Mountain. He had climbed it many times since his grandfather passed. These hidden caves… he didn't know why he thought he might find Agent Gryffin here. He had done a sweat lodge ceremony to pray and to try and find clarity in the death of Tally's mom. And to find Agent Gryffin. He briefly thought back to two days before when Gryffin had collapsed at the scene, where they had medevacked him out of the dessert and to the hospital in Flagstaff. He wasn't sure if Gryffin was having a seizure. He closed his eyes, seeing everything from that morning, trying to look at the scene and the crowd the way Gryffin did. He sighed deeply.

And then Gryffin had been kidnaped from the hospital and had been missing 48 hours. The FBI had teams all over the Res, using helicopters, and dogs and satellite pictures. The studio for the suspect was closed up and had been closed for a couple of weeks according to the other shops around it. No use of credit cards, nothing. A ghost. He felt somehow responsible. He realised he had not maintained the necessary level of professionalism with his people. He was Hopi and a marine. But he was also an FBI agent, and he had a job to do.

Tom had carefully packed his own ammunition, dipping each bullet in white ash. He had dipped his backup ammunition too. Then he had visited the Hopi Medicine Man who confirmed what he had thought. The Medicine Man had never been at the meeting with Gryffin. It had been someone else. He had sat with the Medicine Man, and they had spoken about prayers for Gryffin, protection for himself as he went hunting and for his grandfather's guidance and direction.

Tom had begun to understand more about their perp, and following his revelations from his time in prayer, had made the decision to come to the caves. His grandfather had come to him in a dream and stood pointing to Ghost Mountain. So, he had come, through the windstorm, fully armed, ready to face a demon. And this after the thundering rain on the day they had found Tally's mom. The mountain was dry. A sure sign of magic.

At the bottom of the gully, he had found the red truck, half covered with sagebrush and pieces of cottonwood, blown by the wind, and revealed at the bottom of the trail. There was blood and smeared paint and some kind of oil on the seats. Even if he had needed confirmation, which he didn't, he took it as another sign of being on the right track.

Tom heard the whinny of another horse and turned to see Tally on her mother's mare coming toward him. He nodded at her and waited until she had pulled up next to him. He looked up at her. She was wearing her uniform and gun with a bandana around her face and her hat low on her head. She came beside him, and he looked up into her eyes, his hand on her boot in the stirrup. Speech was impossible and he nodded with his head further up the trail and she nodded back to him.

Tom remounted and started up the last dogleg of the trail that ended at an outcropping of rock with a thin edge. It had taken them twenty minutes just to get to the slim ridge. They were able to fasten the reigns of the horses to a scrub cottonwood and then Tom headed around the rocks to a smaller deer trail that went up a small crevasse in the mountain. The horses nervously nickered when he and Tally passed around the boulder and went out of sight.

It was impossible to see if anyone had come this way as the mountain trail was swept by the wind. It was impossible to see more than a couple of feet in front of them. It was impossible to hear if anyone was ahead of them.

But Tom was listening to the spirit of his grandfather, leading him, letting him know that the cave ahead of him, the one he had discovered on his journey as a child, and later as an adult, was occupied. He also knew evil waited for him in the cave. A *yee naaldlooshii* of terrible power, anger, and hatred.

He stopped on the trail and turned to Tally and held his hand out to her to help her up the last steep part of the trail and into the mouth of the cave. Into hell.

Chapter Twenty-Six

Hege sat with SSA Mike Dubrowski watching the security tapes from the hospital. There was a clear view of someone on a ladder, tipping the camera in the hall to radiology and turning it up, so that anyone going close to the wall could not be identified. Hege sat back. Gryffin could clearly be seen in the wheelchair going into the elevator and the back of the head of the man who must have dosed him and then carried him out the service entrance to a waiting truck, throwing him roughly in the seat, leaving a trail of blood drops from the torn IV according to the other CCTV.

"See, nothing." Agent Dubrowski said again to Hege. Hege had already reviewed the hospital tapes and already knew that nothing was clear on the tapes.

"And traffic cams?"

"We followed the truck to AZ-40 and then north on AZ-89 but lost him after that. We don't know if he went onto the Res or to the Grand Canyon. He could be in Canada by now. Or his body could be…"

Hege shot him a look of such venom that Dubrowski shivered. "Let's not count Agent Gryffin out just yet. He's not only intelligent, he's a marine, he's a survivor."

"You know, I'm still not sure who you are and what your relationship is to SSA Gryffin?" Dubrowski asked again. He had received a phone call from a supervisor and then from another supervisor who told him to give Ms. Andreason anything and everything she wanted without asking questions.

"As I told you before, it's classified," Hege said. "Show me the grid map you're working on."

Dubrowski shrugged and stood up, leading her into a room full of agents, working behind computers, working a phone bank, and others going through paperwork. There was a large map held by magnets to a whiteboard, "Right now, we're hampered by this freak windstorm. Can't see anything out there." Several grids were marked and x'd through. Hege checked the areas visually when her phone buzzed in her pocket.

"Yes."

Dubrowski looked at her curiously.

"You're sure?" She hung up and held her hand out to Dubrowski, "Thank you for your time agent, Dubrowski."

He shook her hand. "Did you get a lead?"

Hege smiled. "We'll be in touch."

He watched the blonde beauty with the scar on her jaw quickly leave the office and head for the elevators. "Jim," he motioned to a young FBI man who was hovering over another agent's shoulder. He quickly ran over to Agent Dubrowski.

"Follow her downstairs and get a license plate off her vehicle."

The young agent ran after Hege to catch her at the elevator.

Chapter Twenty-Seven

Gryffin started to come around with a deep groan. He lay on his side and tried sitting up. His mouth was covered with a gag that he at first thought was cloth but was instead made from leather. He was no longer in the gown from the hospital. He was naked and shivering. His hands were tied with leather thongs behind his back. He knew he was inside a cave from the feel of the ground beneath him, the echo and the darkness of the rock wall behind him. The area he was in had conflicting odours. He smelled sage, creosote, some kind of mushroom or fungus, the smell of bat guano. And cologne. It lingered on his skin. He felt he might be sick and prayed that he wouldn't vomit and choke with the gag in his mouth. His throat was raw, and his head was pounding like he was hungover. In the dark, he could see a low flickering flame as from an open fire, blurrily, not clear at all. Then he realised in that moment, he could at least see light and dark.

Someone was moving in the cave, but their footsteps were muffled. Moccasins? Bare feet? The figure was moving back and forth in front of the fire. There was a heavy smell of smoke in the air too. The smoke seemed familiar to him. Opium? Cannabis? And maybe, cedar? He was struggling to clear his brain to think. His thoughts were scattered and jumbled. His hands were tied behind his back. His knees were tied. His feet were tied.

His legs ached and he realised his knees and feet were also tied with the same leather thongs. He shivered as he tried quietly to test the strength of his bonds. They were tied very well. How long had he been there? He knew there was blood and scabs on his wrists, knees and feet. Every muscle in his body ached and he bore several cuts across his ribs and scrapes on his hips and thighs as if he had been dragged over the ground. He shook his head to try and clear it a little, but it only made it worse. He tried remembering his Corp Survival training. Anything.

Don't panic.

Hallucinogenic. The word came to him. Yes, he was experiencing traces of light. Was he coming down or going up? He tried to get his mind to work. What were the effects? Peyote. Yes, he smelled sage. The Navajo church used peyote. How long… he looked towards the fire and the light began to morph and to change into geometric patterns, until the light was like prisms: rainbow images dancing before his eyes.

The logical part of his mind moved aside, and he began to taste the colours in his mouth. Sunshine, the taste of Mary, ocean waters, salmon, and rivers… time seemed to slow, and he felt like he was floating. The light continued to change into crystals in all the colours filling the cave, falling down the walls, dancing all around him.

Gryffin thought that dark hands lifted him to stand. And freed his hands, knees and feet with a very sharp knife nicking part of his skin and yet he stood motionless. He tasted the music which tasted like colours in the rainbow until tears coursed down his cheeks. He was so moved by the beauty in them. His heart beat with the soft drumbeats. He began to sway and moved his feet a little, side to side. He thought he was sweating but wasn't sure as a cold breeze went over his body and suddenly, he was flying, up and up into the night sky, a night sky filled with the brightest lights he had ever seen. A kaleidoscope of ice and water, with so many colours that he was overwhelmed.

The light usually hurt his eyes but now it was as if he were the light and he was breathing every star into his lungs, and he thought that they would surely burst inside him with the sharp-edged light. His mouth finally relaxed as he felt the restriction fall away but he still couldn't speak. His tongue was fat and lazy. He was grateful, so grateful because a cup was at his lips and the voice, the voice of God was telling him to drink. At first, he was grateful for the liquid, but then the bitterness made his stomach lurch, but still the cup bit into his lips and he had to swallow until he felt as if he were drowning beneath the surface of dark waves.

He was sobbing, his face held in his hands, he was falling in darkness to a bottomless pit until he could not cry out anymore. He hit the ground and he bounced. Pain and darkness surrounded him, and he felt bereft. He was certain he was leaving his body. He was dying. And then from very far away, a small light began to come to his aching eyes. White light, surrounded with all the colours and shades of red waving in a slight breeze, strands reaching out to him in warmth and safety. A face formed with deep green eyes and a beautiful face, pink lips delicate and parted. He heard from very, very far away the sound of music that slowly morphed into language.

It was his name; someone was calling his name. He tried to move towards it, tried to move his hand to touch the face, so brilliant in the light, so beautiful in its warmth. It grew and grew until he felt he was within it, and it was surrounding him. He felt cocooned inside a place of warmth and love and safety. And at that moment, he felt the angel was showing him God. His shoulders and head fell back against a sandy floor, and he fell into oblivion thinking death was nothing to be feared.

Chapter Twenty-Eight

Hege had called in a lot of favours for this. She stood in a desert jeep fully equipped for a war zone. She wore a camo cap with goggles and a long-sleeved camo shirt and pants. She was grateful because the wind was cutting up so that the sand blew almost horizontally. The jeeps, equipped to go at a good clip through the desert were crawling along as visibility was less than twenty feet.

There were five jeeps loaded with experienced, combat mercenaries. Many were close personal friends. She looked at her military-grade, portable GPS. They were close to a trail: a horse trail, which led up Ghost Mountain. They'd have to leave the jeeps and climb the mountain, hoping to be able to discern the trail, find the caves...

'*This is not impossible,*' she told herself for the hundredth time. She could see her crew patiently sitting in the jeeps as they ploughed a narrow path so they wouldn't end up tumbling down some arroyo in the middle of nowhere. The drivers were the best; not far now.

If Hege were a praying woman, she would pray. As it was, she worried for Mary, for her fragile mental health, for Rick's if his sister couldn't function, for herself because Hege had become attached to this group. It was more than a job. It was a lifeline for her, and her mind raced ahead to what they were dealing with. Gryffin was a marine. He would survive. But what kind of shape would they find him in?

She had taken the medicine bag from the floor of the elevator and had immediately sent it to a lab. The material was permeated with Trimethoxyphenethylamine. Mescaline in a pure and potent form. Coupled with Psilocybe cubensis or magic mushrooms and possibly Ecstasy. The medicine bag contained remnants of capsules which would have been activated by Gryffin's sweat and the fact that he kept touching it while it hung around his neck. It had taken some time for the capsules to burst and finally soak into his skin through the cloth of the medicine bag. It was no wonder he had passed out at the crime scene. Tom had also said he thought Gryffin might have had a seizure.

One person on her team was one of the best field medics in the service. She was as prepared as she could be for whatever they were going to find. '*Just let him still be alive.*' She thought, '*For Mary.*'

Chapter Twenty-Nine

Tom and Tally had reached the mouth of the cave. Tally immediately removed her hat and utility belt, holding them in her hand. At this entrance, it was necessary for them to enter by turning their bodies sideways. Tom knew there were other entrances lower down the mountain, but you had to really know the cave to enter or exit them. The cave had many chambers and hundreds of ancillary paths. Some led into other caverns, others led to nothing, blocked by limestone blocks, and somewhere, deep in the mountain were ancient caves with petroglyphs and cave drawings. They were considered sacred by the Tewa and were never discussed with outsiders. There were rooms of tufa, caliche, chalk and micrite. Colourful, sacred, powerful and magical to the Hopi and Navajo.

As he stepped into the cavern, far enough for Tally to be beside him, he realised her weapon was drawn. He allowed his eyes to adjust to the interior and saw a fire burning about 50 feet away from them. He smelled Marijuana, peyote, vomit, and creosote. He didn't see anyone, but he leaned out his spirit into the cave and felt a presence. And not a good one.

Tom and Tally took out flashlights, lined them up with their weapons and split at the mouth of the cave, each taking a different direction. Tom moved around the fire and saw three paths leading to the right. He remembered the first was a dead end. The second led to a larger room and the third led down into the earth. He eased himself to the first entrance, shining his flashlight on the floor of the cave. There were no footprints in the sand going into the path.

Tally had moved towards a darkened floor to the left of the cave entrance, her flashlight shined over the body of Agent Gryffin. His strong young body was naked, covered in dirt, blood, and vomit. She came close to him, shining her light around the room and into corners before kneeling down next to him and feeling at his neck for a pulse.

At first, she thought he was dead as she could not discern a pulse. Then a slow shadow of a pulse went through his veins. His body was slick with some kind of oil and paint. Tally absentmindedly wiped it on her pant leg. She rolled him onto his back. His face was a mask of horror and terror, marked with paint and sweat. There was no sign of recognition in his eyes, only empty blue with huge, dilated pupils. Tally shivered and stood, continuing to clear the cavern looking for their perp.

Tom had moved onto the next path and stood looking down at the entrance. It was clear that a set of moccasins had come in and out of this room. "Tally…" he hissed. She looked at him and he nodded his head in the direction of the room. She nodded, cleared the rest of the wall and the small niches on her side of the cavern, then followed Tom down the path into the larger room. This part of the cave was larger and should be completely black, but as they came to a corner that blocked the room, an eerie light came from the interior of the cave.

Tally recognised it as the light from glow sticks. Hundreds of glow sticks lit the limestone cavern with eerie shadows and fingers of phosphorescent light. This cave must have been made of streaks of calcite and fluorite because it picked up the colours of the glow sticks and amplified them. Tom showed his light around the cave as Tally came to his right side, shining her flashlight in the opposite direction. They could discern nothing other than the cave itself. Tom shook himself as the walls seemed to be talking and he felt as if the cave were alive with spirits. Tally also heard the talking and looked at Tom. "Peyote," she mouthed. Tom nodded absently and turned to leave the cave when Skinwalker, who had been hidden on a ledge above the entrance of the cave, launched himself onto the two Hopi officers.

Skinwalker was naked but for a loincloth, his skin slick with paint, oil and sweat. He was in a complete psychotic mania, screaming and trying to club them both to death. Skinwalker knocked Tom's gun from his hands and Tom drew on his marine training to roll and come back up with a knife from his right ankle. Skinwalker sprung up and rolled on top of Tally knocking her gun and flashlight from her hands and began punching her in the face and had the club raised above his head to strike her when Tom launched himself from a crouch hitting Skinwalker at the ribs, his arms encompassing Skinwalker and rolling with him on the floor of the cave.

Tally was up in a moment on her hands and knees, scouring the floor of the cave with her hands for her weapon. The minute her hand touched her weapon she heard a grunt and then the sound of someone being clubbed and she turned and looked in horror to see Skinwalker on top of Tom, Tom's body inert and Tom's knife sticking out of Skinwalker's ribs. The club was coming down on Tom when Tally squeezed the trigger to her gun, the sound echoing in the cave so loud it hurt her ears. Skinwalker slumped sideways, his body still. Tally held her breath as Skinwalker coughed and then rolled over and stood up, moving fast.

Tally got another shot off, but it ricocheted and pinged around the cave making her dive down to the floor for cover. Expecting a blow to the head she rolled over and found that Skinwalker had left the cave. She scrambled to her feet and crossed the room to Tom on her hands and knees. One side of his head was bleeding badly, and his eyes were just beginning to drift open.

"Tom," she said in a hard whisper.

"Tom, we got to move." She shook him again and he came up suddenly. He rolled to all fours and Tally sat back on her heels, anxious to get out of the cavern and after Skinwalker. Tom spit a couple of times and then put his right arm out and Tally grabbed it helping him to his feet.

He stopped and felt down his left leg for his backup piece and pulled it from the holster, while Tally retrieved one of the flashlights. The other was broken, so Tom grabbed a couple of the glow sticks and put them in his jacket pocket and followed Tally out of the cavern. He hung back as she cleared the entrance, and they came into the large room.

There was no sign of Skinwalker but there was a trail of blood leading across the cave to another of the entrances. One that Tom had not been down to. Tally shined the light to the darkened floor where Agent Gryffin had been lying. His body was gone. Tally ground her teeth in frustration. "He's got Gryffin, damn it! Let's go!"

Chapter Thirty

Hege's Team had found the red truck, and now had reached the trail heading up the mountain. They were on foot in a single line coming up the narrow path. The lead tracker held his hand up in a fist, lowered his weapon and started chuckling. Further up the trail, he came up to Tom and Tally's horses who were whickering at the company, having grown nervous in the wind and from the lack of humans. Hege moved through the group checking the horses.

"Looks like Tom Evehema's horse. I'm not sure about the other."

One of the men was looking through the saddlebags of the other horse.

"Looks like an Officer Talayumptewa. They both must be in the cave."

Hege tapped him on the shoulder. "OK Tracker. Let's go. Be advised, looking for two males and one female, friendly. One bogie."

The horses whinnied in anxiety at being left again, as the soldiers and Hege moved up the trail single file to the mouth of the cave. They realised quickly they would have to remove their gear to get through the entrance. With military precision and symbiotic movements, they moved as quickly as possible, only sending two at a time through the entrance of the cave.

Chapter Thirty-One

Mary pulled the kneeler from the seat in front of her in the chapel at the hospital. She brought her hands together as she had been taught when she was a child, bowed her head, and closed her eyes. She didn't know any prayers. But she reached out with her spirit to God, any god. The words tumbled from her mind in flashes of her time with Gryffin: the first moment they met at the FBI offices in Seattle, his attention on her at every book signing and through the trials of her first encounter of violence with her stalker in the Pike Marketplace. She had been saved by Justis Smith, a cop who would not give up. She lifted Justis's name up, hoping he could help. Her mind raced through her short relationship with Gryffin remembering his hands on her, kissing her, loving her. She missed him like breath and air. Pleading without words, until the air was heavy around her, and breathing was difficult, she broke down.

Behind her, two team members watched as she began to weep, and then sob until her body was shaking. Each man was affected by her sorrow, but incapable of helping her. The candles fluttered on the altar and from somewhere music began to play softly in the background. It was the Kyrie Eleison, in Latin, sung without instruments, the voices echoing in the small chapel. The chapel filled with soft sounds, voices ethereal and unreal to her. She saw only blackness before her even though it seemed full of colours kaleidoscoping and hovering around the periphery of her vision. She felt out of her body and miles away from the chapel.

Slowly, Mary came to herself and then sat back on the wooden pew, exhausted and wiping her cheeks with the back of her hand. She pulled a tissue from a box sitting on the seat. She began to focus on the stained-glass window in front of her, her spirit settling and finally accepting the momentary peace provided. She sat in silence, not moving, only holding the likeness of Gryffin in her mind, his smile, the way he looked at her, touched her, loved her… and she began to weep again in long sighing sobs.

Chapter Thirty-Two

Gryffin realised through a haze that he was being roughly hauled to his feet. Nothing in his mind could get his body to work. Everything around him was black and the air was alive and breathing, breathing heavily near his ear. His body was slick with sweat, his feet bloody and bruised yet he was being pulled deeper and deeper into the blackness. He began to whimper, not knowing if it was his voice or not. He thought there were creatures, black creatures all around him, pulling at his body, pulling his mind out of his head. He wanted to scream but couldn't make a sound other than whimpering. At one point he tried to pull back, to stop the ever downward spiral he felt he was falling into.

A hand came from the dark and roughly slapped him across the face. He smelled blood, vomit, and sage. His face was oily and slick and, as he stumbled along, he oddly remembered the Kyrie from the church when he was little. It seemed in his mind the voices of the chant were coming from all parts of the cave, all parts of the darkness, filling his senses, lifting his soul. Was this what it was like: was he dying and ascending? Why did he keep feeling the pain in his body, the ache of his joints, the blinding pain in his head if he was dead?

The air around him kept breathing harder and harder when finally it stopped and stumbled. He was falling over the body of another person. Was he in purgatory? Were there other bodies falling and bumping together in darkness, in Perpetua? In utter silence, he felt himself sinking into the dirt floor, confused, and then accepting his place on the hard packed earth and sand. He was so tired. Sinking, sinking into utter darkness.

From a long, long place away from him, he heard voices, calling his name. Was it the angels? Were angels calling him home? It was so dark, and he felt so utterly lost in the blackness, so utterly alone. The Kyrie began to rise up again in him. He felt the music soothing his broken skin, his aching body, his pounding head. He felt himself being lifted in the arms of an angel. The angel had multicoloured lights coming out of its side, its right side.

Was it Christ who had come for him? The face was coming closer, and he knew he should recognise it. It was illuminated with flashes of light, and he felt the strength in the angel's arms, tasting blood. He felt the communion of body and soul, feeling immersed in the body of Christ before the ecstasy of Christ overwhelmed him and he stopped breathing.

Chapter Thirty-Three

It was slow going. With Tom in the lead, and Tally following, they could clearly see the blood trail, the dragging footsteps that had to be Agent Gryffin. They would come to places where the floor of the cave was hard packed, and they would have to retrace their steps and try to pick up the trail again. Tom deliberately dropped glow sticks at intervals so he could find his way back up in case they got lost. They only had one flashlight between them. Blood ran down the side of his face and he kept swiping at it with the back of his hand.

Tom's head throbbed and his vision was blurred from the concussion, but he heard his grandfather's voice, encouraging him, telling him to keep going and so he found that strength within himself to keep pushing on, despite the hallucinations and echoes of the cave. He reached his hand behind him to grab Tally's hand, connecting them both for courage and strength.

The further they recessed into the caves, the darker it was and the more they heard the voices reaching out to them. It felt as if the single light from Tally's flashlight would never be enough. Both Tally and Tom were beginning to feel the effects of the Peyote based oil. Skinwalker must have been coated in it when Tom and he wrestled on the floor because it was all over Tom's face and hands, hands that had touched Tally.

At some point, Tom started to shout Gryffin's name into the chambers, panic had begun to take root, the darkness that surrounded them was becoming too overwhelming. Both he and Tally called out, moved forward, called out again and then moved forward again and again, following the drops of blood, the taste of it in their mouths, their ancestors leading them in the prismed light from their single flashlight, guiding them, giving them strength and courage when they had reached a state of exhaustion. The glow sticks took on a life of their own, colours looping like music around them swirling at their feet. They pressed on, encouraging and holding one another up.

Suddenly they came to a juncture in the path and there were two bodies: one dark, one light, both naked, tangled in blood and sand on the floor in front of them.

Chapter Thirty-Four

Hege's team had to remove their gear to enter the mouth of the cave without making a larger opening. Once inside, they quickly explored the front cave and found traces of blood and scuff marks. Hege and her guys had to stand for a moment blinking at all the glow sticks placed methodically around the second cave.

"How the hell did he get up there? There's no ladder, no scaffolding." Scout looked down at the floor. "Blood and a struggle in here," one of the team told Hege. Hege quickly turned to look at the entrance to the cave and showed her flashlight along the ledge above the door.

"Ledges carved into the rock. With the shadows, you would have to know they were there. Let's keep going." They exited the room and the team equipped with weapons that had laser sights and night vision goggles equipped began to sweep the room.

"Here!"

Another one of the team was standing on the sandy, bloody floor of the main cavern.

"We had a body here, looks like it was dragged or carried out of here, this way." Quickly they went into the first three paths and quickly cleared them.

They formed a single line following each other down the path halting only for one or two to try and follow any footprints in the sand or hard rock. They tried to move fast but it was still slow going trying to eliminate false paths.

"We have two maybe three bleeders."

It was the next report as they cautiously headed at a downward angle sharper than the others. Suddenly, the lead stopped and put up his fist for them all to halt. From up ahead of them, they heard someone shouting a name. The name was 'Gryffin'. And it echoed through the cavern… a desperate, pleading sound.

"Double-time," Hege stated unnecessarily as the team started moving at a run.

Hege's army came around a corner and found the body of Skinwalker. They immediately halted and Hege moved to the front. She turned the head of the serial killer, "That's our Bogie."

"Not our man," Scout spoke to the group. "Keep going. There will be three friendlies, let's remember that."

They quickly kept moving ahead through the cave following a new pattern of blood drops.

Chapter Thirty-Five

Tom clutched the body of Gryffin close to his chest as he descended into the last part of the path that went toward a small exit of the cave. Tom stumbled slightly and Tally had her arms around him and loosely under Gryffin's feet. She pulled them back into her arms. They were both breathing hard. She could feel how cold Gryffin's body was. Tally's face was slick with tears, the drug laden oil and blood.

"Tom, he's not breathing. Stop, put him down."

Tom was evidently going into shock; he was cold and there was blood dripping from his side.

"Tom, listen to me, he's not breathing. Put him down," Tally pleaded.

Carefully lowering his burden to the ground in the small space around them, Tally straightened Gryffin's body on the small path and began CPR. Tally could taste the peyote and vomit in Gryffin's mouth. She persevered and then Tom took over for a few minutes. Suddenly they heard the noises from the men coming down the path above them and they both froze as they saw light from laser sites hitting the ceiling and walls. When Tom picked up Gryffin, he had lain his gun on the cave floor. Neither of them had a weapon. Suddenly the path was filled with mercenaries.

Standing at the top of the path behind them all was a six foot something Danish goddess.

"Medic!" was all she said.

Chapter Thirty-Six

When they all exited the cave, they couldn't believe what they were seeing. The sandstorm had completely passed; the sun was shining down on them as they pulled the litter containing Agent Gryffin's body out of the caves. They could hear the whirl of helicopter blades above them and hear the horses whinnying in panic above. It was a shock to their bodies after the darkness of the caves.

The litter bearers, along with Hege, carried a bag of saline that was hard-lined into Gryffin's arm. They knelt and turned their faces away from the wash from the rotor blades until the helicopter had touched down. Then they sprinted for the door, which was already opening, where two paramedics leapt out to help move the litter into the helicopter and began to load. Hege turned to Scout and nodded and then climbed aboard the chopper and the door slammed.

The rest of the crew moved back, bending low and keeping their faces away from the chopper's wash. When the chopper had gone, they stood up and patted each other on the backs. At that moment, Tom and Tally stumbled out of the cave entrance and into the light, blinking like a couple of moles coming above ground.

The lead walked up to Tally because she was wearing a uniform.

"You need help recovering that body?"

She looked at him for a brief moment, her eyes unfocused, uncomprehending, swaying and then she nodded. The medic had Tom sitting on a boulder, while another man went up the trail to retrieve the horses. She turned back to the hidden entrance they had crawled out of. The lead looked at her and felt a wave of compassion go through him. "We can do it. Why don't you stay here with your friend? We'll bring the body out."

She hesitated a moment and then lowered her head and took a deep breath.

"No, I'll go with you. It's my job."

"We recovered your weapons. I have them secure."

The lead straightened his pack and nodded. Tally straightened her shoulders and walked back to the small entrance with the lead and three of his men, who followed her back into the caves.

Chapter Thirty-Seven

One of Mary's security guards lifted his hand to his ear. There was a light beep and Mary turned around. "They've found his b…"

Mary was too afraid to stand.

"They've located Agent Gryffin. They're getting ready to bring him in. No ETA yet. They'll advise."

Mary sank back down on the wooden pew looking at the window, the altar, the candles. She couldn't focus on anything. She should check her blood sugar. In a moment, even without speaking, one of her guards was beside her on the wooden pew with a bottle of juice in his hands, holding it to her lips.

"Come on, Mary, drink," he instructed patiently.

She drank a little and then looked up into the blue eyes, actually seeing the man for a few moments. She took the bottle in her hands and drank thirstily. "Name."

"Carpenter, ma'am."

"Thanks, Carpenter." He looked away and put a hand to his ear leaning away from her. "They have Agent Gryffin. They're bringing him on a chopper…" he paused as he listened. "You should wait here…"

"No! What's the ETA? How long?"

She was clutching his arm hard.

"ETA is 30 minutes."

"Take me to the roof," Mary said, standing up.

"We have some time, ma'am. Finish your juice."

She looked as if she might argue, but she sat and took the bottle of juice back and began to drink the rest of it, trying to strengthen herself for what was to come. Carpenter stayed beside her, ready to help in any way he could.

Chapter Thirty-Eight

At the junction of AZ-264 and the dirt road leading off to Ghost Mountain, an odd procession was making its way across the canyon floor. Two Hopi mounted on horses, followed by three military jeeps and a team of twelve men. On the last jeep, there was a litter with the body of a serial killer, a Hopi cum Navajo boy who had failed to appease the spirits of his mother and father.

They were met by the FBI, ERTU, an ambulance, the Navajo Nation Police Force, Hopi Law Enforcement, and Chairman of the Council, Tim Nuvangyaoma and most of the council in a conglomeration of jeeps, trucks, and vans. When the horses pulled up in front of Tim Nuvangyaoma, both Tom and Tally dismounted and walked to him: bruised and bloody and bandaged, but standing tall. Tom looked up into the Chairman's eyes and said, "He is dead. We have retrieved the body. It is over."

Tim Nuvangyaoma held his hand out to Tom, and Tom, dumbfounded, took the hand and shook it. Tim smiled at him and patted his arm.

"Welcome home."

Tom, blood still seeping from his face and marking his shirt, felt intense emotion rise up in him. He swallowed deeply and nodded. Then Tim Nuvangyaoma turned to Tally and saluted her. She stood rigid and with an imperceptible nod of her head, rested her hand on her utility belt and looked down the line of council members and others from her village. A sense of pride and ownership ran through her blood and flushed her cheeks, despite her face being battered and her eye swollen on one side.

Coming up AZ-264 was a phalanx of FBI vehicles with sirens going and red lights flashing. The body was transferred to the ERTU unit van and the desert mercenaries made a quick departure up the canyon and away from the FBI. As the FBI arrived on the scene, Tom and Tally's horses were being loaded into horse vans. Behind the FBI was a medic unit that treated them both and then loaded Tom and Tally onto an ambulance to go to Flagstaff hospital for observation.

The Hopi and Navajo quickly moved off the road and returned to their respective homes.

The FBI left with the ERTU unit.

A single gust of wind blew across the highway, a dust devil spinning lazily in the hot sun.

Chapter Thirty-Nine

Mary stood on the roof waiting for the chopper to land, Carpenter standing close behind her. Her long red hair whipped about her face, her dress moulding to her body, her hands twisting together, shaking. Behind her were two more security guards and a very angry hospital guard. They all ducked as the chopper came in for a landing and the doors opened. Carpenter sheltered Mary's body with his own. As a gurney came out of the helipad bay doors, the team from the hospital of doctors and nurses rushed to the helicopter.

Hege leapt out of the helicopter and began to walk towards Mary. Mary began to cry aloud and collapsed, Carpenter stepped up putting his arms around her from behind, lifting her back onto her feet. The paramedic team was already doing CPR which continued while a nurse climbed onto Gryffin's chest taking over CPR from the paramedics as the gurney was rapidly wheeled into the hospital, one paramedic holding Gryffin's IV.

Hege raised her arms to Mary and somehow Mary ran into them sobbing. Carpenter followed her with his eyes, the wind from the rotor blowing his dark hair.

Chapter Forty

Tom Evehema stood on the edge of First Mesa, looking out over the beautiful desert blooming after the huge rainstorm. It was dawn, and the dessert was painted in rosy colours marking new life and hope. His hair was getting longer, and it brushed against his collar in the morning breeze. As the sun rose, the colours became more vibrant and the lines of the rocks in the mesas more clearly defined. He breathed the clean air and scents of the desert, sage and creosote, mesquite, and flowering cactus. The sky was going to be clear and cloudless, and the mountains were framed against it beautifully.

His heart was heavy in his chest, but as he took another deep breath, he knew that he was Hopi. A part of his ancestral line and his blood sang while looking over the dessert. The conflicts that he had in his life resolved into the man he was now. He had made peace with his choices and knew in his heart he was doing what he was supposed to be doing. Representing his tribe and his country. This is where he was born, and this is where he would serve. His job was to help lead, support and be there for his tribe, for the Hopi Nation.

He turned away and walked across the main square to the kiva, carefully fitting his tall frame into the small opening and climbing down the ladder into the dark interior. Tally was already seated next to the medicine woman, her long dark hair a curtain hiding her face. Silently, he walked towards them and sat cross-legged on the floor. He took a deep breath and stilled his mind and allowed the moment to infuse his spirit and calm his soul, focusing only on his inner self.

They had come to mourn together, these childhood friends, the loss of their family and good friends. A small burner filled with cedar sat in front of them and the chanting began with the medicine woman. A small amount of tobacco was sprinkled over the fire and its pungent scent filled the kiva.

The medicine woman asked them to picture the faces of the lost. She paused after each name was said to allow their spirits to enter the room, to be honoured, remembered, loved and let go. Their spirits could rise and be released from the First Mesa and from the surrounding villages. The drums and singers began to play. Tom had not even seen them in the darkened corners, but he knew they were there. He felt his own spirit rise above him, floating to the ceiling as the faces passed in his mind. His deep sense of loss and grief was overwhelming at first but as the ancestral chant for healing the soul was sung, he eventually heard his spirit lift with the flute's sad and plaintive notes.

Tally's mind was full of visions and memories of her mother. Her mother's beautiful face laughing with her, fierce in her defence of her daughter, walking in the corn fields, watching as Tally was pinned with her badge for the first time, her mother brushing her long hair and singing to her while she braided Tally's hair. Tally began to weep quietly until her shoulders and entire body began to shake.

Tally was sobbing quietly near him, and he moved closer to her, to put his arm around her. She was stiff for a few moments, before leaning into him. He stroked her hair with his hand, rocked her in his arms while the Kiva filled with the sound of the flute, piping sad and gentle through the high desert air. The scent of cedar and sage filled their heads with the images of loving faces sharing laughter and joy. Those images rose like smoke into the beautiful blue sky, fading into the valleys and mesas. Spirits freed from pain and fear, death, and destruction, to be at peace and come into the company of their ancestors.

The music had long stopped, and the kiva was silent. Tom felt a shift in the air and was loath to let go of Tally. Tom opened his eyes to see that they were alone. The others had quietly left, allowing them to come up at their own pace. After a bit, Tally quieted and then drew away from Tom wiping the tears from her face. He pulled an old hanky from his back pocket and wordlessly offered it to her. She took it from his hands to blow her nose and finish wiping the tears from her cheeks.

"Are you ready to go up?" he asked quietly.

She looked around the kiva and then back at him. A smile flitted across her features. She lifted her hand to his cheek and held it for a moment. He lifted his hand to her cheek, and they sat looking into each other's eyes, for a moment until their hands fell away. Tom stood and reached a hand down to her, to help lift her up. They both had been sitting so long they were unsteady. As Tally stood, she stumbled and fell forward into his arms.

It was the most natural thing to do, to pull her into his arms and kiss her forehead, her cheeks, her lips, for the kiss to deepen; and like that, all the terror, danger and fear that had bound them before was replaced with love, care, concern and grace, filling them until a greater peace settled on them as they broke apart. He held her hand as they walked up to the ladder to the roof. At the bottom, he pulled her back into his arms again, kissing her thoroughly, until she giggled like a young woman again beneath him; wriggling away to turn and climb the ladder and re-enter their world, their sacred community, their sacred land and into the world of the living.

Epilogue

All things considered, it was not what he expected to happen, but nonetheless, he was happy with the result. Once again, Mary was alone, save her hero brother, her security guards, her fans. This put her in a perfect position as far as he was concerned. But this was a situation to be savoured. This was a situation not to be rushed but tended carefully like a garden.

The old nursery rhyme flitted through his head… Mary, Mary, quite contrary, how does your garden grow? He chuckled to himself. Quite a garden Miss Mary was growing. Bodies in graves were such a pretty garden, topped with graveyard flowers. Would she leave roses for Gryffin? And if so, what colour would they be?

It was true he hated her when she wore black. Black was not her colour. She looked better in red. Blood red. Perhaps he would send her a silk blouse, to replace the one she lost. He still had shreds of it in his tackle box.

In red, of course.

Milton Keynes UK
Ingram Content Group UK Ltd.
UKHW021032141123
432541UK00011B/96